EX LIBRIS

VINTAGE CLASSICS

D1627840

THINGS: A STORY OF THE SIXTIES WITH A MAN ASLEEP

Georges Perec (1936-82) won the Prix Renaudot in 1965 for his first novel *Things: A Story of the Sixties*, and went on to exercise his unrivalled mastery of language in almost every imaginable kind of writing, from the apparently trivial to the deeply personal. He composed acrostics, anagrams, autobiography, criticism, crosswords, descriptions of dreams, film scripts, heterograms, lipograms, memories, palindromes, plays, poetry, radio plays, recipes, riddles, stories short and long, travel notes, univocalics, and, of course, novels. *Life A User's Manual*, which draws on many of Perec's other works, appeared in 1978 after nine years in the making and was acclaimed a masterpiece to put beside Joyce's *Ulysses*. It won the Prix Médicis and established Perec's international reputation.

David Bellos, the translator of *Things: A Story of the Sixties*, is Professor of French and Comparative Literature and Director of the Program in Translation and Intercultural Communication at Princeton University.

In 2005 David Bellos was awarded the Man Booker International Translator's Prize for his many translations of the novels of the distinguished Albanian writer Ismail Kadare. He is the author of several works on Balzac, the prize-winning biography *Georges Perec: A Life in Words*, and a biography of Romain Gary, published in 2010.

GEORGES PEREC

Things

A Story of the Sixties

TRANSLATED FROM THE FRENCH BY
David Bellos

with

A Man Asleep

TRANSLATED FROM THE FRENCH BY
Andrew Leak

WITH AN INTRODUCTION BY
David Bellos

VINTAGE BOOKS
London

Published by Vintage 2011

2 4 6 8 10 9 7 5 3 1

Things: A Story of the Sixties first published in France with the title *Les Choses*
in 1965 by Editions Julliard
A Man Asleep first published in France with the title *Un homme qui dort*
in 1967 by Editions Denoël

First published in Great Britain in 1990 by Collins Harvill
This edition first published in 1999 by the Harvill Press

Vintage
Random House, 20 Vauxhall Bridge Road,
London SW1V 2SA

www.vintage-classics.info

Addresses for companies within The Random House Group Limited
can be found at: www.randomhouse.co.uk/offices.htm

The Random House Group Limited Reg. No. 954009

A CIP catalogue record for this book
is available from the British Library

ISBN 9780099541660

The Random House Group Limited supports The Forest
Stewardship Council (FSC), the leading international forest
c~~ertification organisation. All our titles that are printed~~ on
G~~reen~~ ~~FSC certified paper carry the FSC l~~ogo.

CONTENTS

INTRODUCTION

GEORGES PEREC was born in Paris in 1936, and his memories of early childhood and of the war years, some of which he spent as a refugee in the French Alps, are recorded in chapters of *W or The Memory of Childhood* (1975). He was educated in Paris and at a state boarding school at Etampes, then at the Lycée Henri-IV and the Sorbonne, where he followed courses in history and sociology for two years without much enthusiasm. He did two years' military service in a parachute regiment but was exempted from active service in Algeria. After a year spent in Sfax (Tunisia) and a short period working as a market researcher, Perec obtained a post of archivist in a medical research laboratory in Paris in 1962, and he remained employed in the same capacity until 1979. He died in March 1982 after a short illness.

Perec decided to be a writer before he was twenty, but, for nearly ten years, apart from a few book reviews and essays on literature and film, he published nothing. *Things. A Story of the Sixties* was his first book and it made him famous almost instantly. *A Man Asleep* followed just over a year later, but created much less of a stir. These two short novels are published here in English together because, more than any other of Perec's numerous and very diverse writings, they shed light on each other, represent the two different sides of something like the same coin.

Things. A Story of the Sixties was begun in 1962 under

7

the title "The Great Adventure" but did not reach its final form until 1964. It was published in September 1965 as *Les Choses. Une histoire des années soixante*, in the "Lettres nouvelles" collection edited by Maurice Nadeau for Julliard, and was an immediate success, selling far more copies than first novels by unknown authors usually do. The award of the Renaudot prize, some two months later, confirmed, rather than created, the perception of *Things* as the story of a whole generation. By the end of the 1960s, it had been translated into most European languages and had found its place on French literature syllabuses throughout the world. Student editions in French were published both in Moscow and in New York; it has since also become a set text in French secondary schools.

As is often the case with works of European literature, *Things* fared less well in the English-speaking world than almost anywhere else. It was at least translated (by Helen Lane) in the 1960s, but the Grove Press edition (now a bibliographic rarity) was hardly reviewed at all and was never even issued in Britain. The text published here is an entirely new translation.

Superficially, both *Things. A Story of the Sixties* and *A Man Asleep* bear a family resemblance to the kind of *avant-garde* fiction which was, by the mid-sixties, no longer quite as new as the term "new novel" suggested. Neither of Perec's books has a strong narrative structure; neither has strongly delineated characters. But the use Perec made of what now looks like a period style is very different from the fiction of Alain Robbe-Grillet or Michel Butor, and opens a new and far more accessible chapter in the history of the novel.

Things aims to exhaust all that can be said about *fascination*, and, more particularly, to explore what words like *happiness* and *freedom* can mean in the modern world – the world of consumerism as it was emerging in the France of de Gaulle. *A Man Asleep* is a similarly exhaustive exploration of its opposite, indifference. Both novels seem to arise from the banal but no less poignant contradiction between feelings of being and not being in the world.

Both these novels were written before Perec had any contact with the Ouvroir de littérature potentielle, or OuLiPo – indeed, before OuLiPo was known outside of a tiny circle. Although they are not generated by formal mechanisms of the kind used for *Life A User's Manual*, they are nonetheless highly crafted, constructed texts. *Things*, Perec said in a lecture at the University of Warwick, was written to fill the blank space created, so to speak, by the juxtaposition of four works of importance to him: Roland Barthes' *Mythologies*; Flaubert's *Sentimental Education*; Paul Nizan's *La Conspiration*; and a striking account of life in the concentration camps, Robert Antelme's *L'Espèce humaine*. *A Man Asleep* (its title taken from Proust's *Remembrance of Things Past*) is constructed more literally from its six progenitory models; Kafka, Melville, Lowry, Proust, Le Clézio, Joyce.

Things. A Story of the Sixties was read, in the 1960s, as a sociological novel, and, very often, as a denunciation of consumer capitalism. That is no doubt why it was so rapidly translated into all the languages of Eastern Europe. For Perec, however, it was not that at all, any more than it was a celebration of its characters' fascination with material wealth. Its main idea, he said, was to explore the way "the language of advertising is reflected in us", whilst describing simply, "in barely heightened terms", the particular social world which happened to be his. The result is a masterpiece of detachment and ambiguity, with an ending that is "neither positive nor negative; you finish on ambiguity; to my mind, it's a happy ending and also the saddest ending you could possibly imagine. . . ." Through his use of a shifting narrator, who is neither "above" his

9

characters looking down on them, as in a traditional novel, nor "inside" them, as in more modern "stream of consciousness" writing, Perec is reaching towards the kind of simultaneous passion and detachment characteristic of Flaubert, and he achieves a mixture of understated affection and discreet irony close to the tone of many of the tales to be told a decade later in *Life A User's Manual*.

A Man Asleep, published in 1967 under the title *Un Homme qui dort*, deals with a depression so extreme as to verge on self-annihilation. The experience is one which Perec says he went through himself around the age of twenty. It is a subject to which he returned, through self-quotation and adaptation, first in the film version of *A Man Asleep*, released in 1974, and then in 1978, in chapter fifty-two of *Life A User's Manual*. In this last variant, the character is given a name, Grégoire Simpson – echoing Kafka's Gregor Samsa (in *The Metamorphosis*), who wakes one morning to find life intolerable in a different way – and he seems to end up throwing himself off a railway bridge. That is no reason for believing that *A Man Asleep* also ends in bleak despair. It ends at Place Clichy, in the rain, waiting for it to stop. A step has been taken towards "waking up" from the sleep of indifference, but there is no guarantee that any number of further steps will take you out of hell, or back into the world of living. Perec's novel brings you only to the brink of carrying on. Like *Things*, and as if to mirror it, *A Man Asleep* ends on an ambiguity which is both moral and literary. Perec not only allows, but obliges his reader to take responsibility for the meaning of the work.

A Man Asleep is a second-person novel. English has no equivalent for the singular, *tu* form of the second person pronoun in French, used by Perec throughout the text. Whereas *vous* is the (plural) polite and formal way of saying "you" in French (and is the form used, for example, in

Michel Butor's second-person narrative of a train journey, *La Modification*), the *tu* form is familiar, friendly, but also (in some circumstances) aggressive. What is also not clear, in the French as in the English, is who, in *A Man Asleep*, is saying *tu* to whom.

In the film version, made by Perec himself together with Bernard Queysanne (after various attempts to turn *Things* into a film had come to nought), a shortened version of the novel is read as a voice-over against images of a young man silently performing the routines of self-effacement described in the text. The voice-over is read by a woman: and the choice of a female voice was made so as to avoid the implication, which a male voice would undoubtedly have had, of the text being the interior monologue of the young man seen on the screen. Is it then the voice of his conscience (a noun of feminine gender in French)? or the voice of "his" mother? or simply a voice distinct from his own? *A Man Asleep*, both as a film and as a novel, merges the two normal poles of communication into one, as if writer and reader (speaker and hearer) had ceased to be separable, but remain distinct from the "character" in the text or on the screen. "The teller of the tale could well be the one to whom the tale is told," Roger Kleman suggested in a review of Perec's novel. "The second person of *A Man Asleep* is the grammatical form of absolute loneliness, of utter deprivation." Of course the reader of the novel, in English translation, may wish to imagine that there is a character in *A Man Asleep* talking to himself, "as in a dream"; but the evidence of the film version shows that Perec did not wish to read his own text in that way.

"The idea of writing the story of my past arose almost at the same time as the idea of writing," Perec states in *W or The Memory of Childhood* (p. 26). The present introduction cannot avoid seeming to give clues (Etampes; Sfax; market research; depression) to the autobiographical content of Perec's twin novels of the nineteen-sixties. However, it would be wrong to assume, just because the material of these stories resembles some of the elements in the real life of Georges Perec, that the main interest of Perec's works is confessional. Autobiography, as readers of *W or The Memory of Childhood* are made to realise, is always fiction; the converse is perhaps not quite as true.

DAVID BELLOS
Manchester, 1989

Quotations unattributed in the text are taken from statements made by Perec in an interview with Marcel Benabou and Bruno Marcenac, published in *Les Lettres françaises*, No. 1108 (2 December 1965), pp. 14–15; and from "Pouvoirs et limites du romancier français contemporain", a lecture given at the University of Warwick in May 1967. Roger Klemans's review of *Un Homme qui dort* was published in *Les Lettres nouvelles*, July/September issue, 1967, pp. 158–166.

THINGS

A STORY OF THE SIXTIES

Translated from the French by
David Bellos

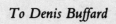

To Denis Buffard

Incalculable are the benefits civilization has brought us, incommensurable the productive power of all classes of riches originated by the inventions and discoveries of science. Inconceivable the marvellous creations of the human sex in order to make men more happy, more free, and more perfect. Without parallel the crystalline and fecund fountains of the new life which still remains closed to the thirsty lips of the people who follow in their griping and bestial tasks.

MALCOLM LOWRY

PART ONE

I

Your eye, first of all, would glide over the grey fitted carpet in the narrow, long and high-ceilinged corridor. Its walls would be cupboards, in light-coloured wood, with fittings of gleaming brass. Three prints, depicting, respectively, the Derby winner Thunderbird, a paddle-steamer named *Ville-de-Montereau*, and a Stephenson locomotive, would lead to a leather curtain hanging on thick, black, grainy wooden rings which would slide back at the merest touch. There, the carpet would give way to an almost yellow woodblock floor, partly covered by three faded rugs.

It would be a living room about twenty-three feet long by ten feet wide. On the left, in a kind of recess, there would be a large sofa upholstered in worn black leather, with pale cherrywood bookcases on either side, heaped with books in untidy piles. Above the sofa, a mariner's chart would fill the whole length of that section of the wall. On the other side of a small low table, and beneath a silk prayer-mat nailed to the wall with three large-headed brass studs, matching the leather curtain, there would be another sofa, at right angles to the first, with a light-brown velvet covering; it would lead on to a small and spindly piece of furniture, lacquered in dark red and providing three display shelves for knick-knacks: agates and stone eggs, snuffboxes, candy-boxes, jade ashtrays, a mother-of-pearl oystershell, a silver fob watch, a cut-glass glass, a crystal pyramid, a miniature in an oval frame. Further on, beyond

21

a padded door, there would be shelving on both sides of the corner, for caskets and for records, beside a closed gramophone of which only four machined-steel knobs would be visible, and above it, a print depicting *The Great Parade of the Military Tattoo*. Through the window, draped with white and brown curtains in cloth imitating Jouy wallpaper, you would glimpse a few trees, a tiny park, a bit of street. A roll-top desk littered with papers and pen-holders would go with a small cane-seated chair. On a console table would be a telephone, a leather diary, a writing pad. Then, on the other side of another door, beyond a low, square revolving bookcase supporting a large, cylindrical vase decorated in blue and filled with yellow roses, set beneath an oblong mirror in a mahogany frame, there would be a narrow table with its two benches upholstered in tartan, which would bring your eye back to the leather curtain.

It would be all in browns, ochres, duns and yellows: a world of slightly dull colours, in carefully graded shades, calculated with almost too much artistry, in the midst of which would be some striking, brighter splashes – a cushion in almost garish orange, a few multicoloured book jackets amongst the leather-bound volumes. During the day, the light flooding in would make this room seem a little sad, despite the roses. It would be an evening room. But in the winter, with the curtains drawn, some spots illuminated – the bookcase corner, the record shelves, the desk, the low table between the two settees, and the vague reflections in the mirror – and large expanses in shadow, whence all the things would gleam – the polished wood, the rich, heavy silks, the cut glass, the softened leather – it would be a haven of peace, a land of happiness.

The first door would open onto a bedroom, its floor covered with a light-coloured fitted carpet. An English double bed would fill the whole rear part of it. On the right, to both sides of the window, there would be tall and narrow sets of shelves holding a few books, to be read and read again, photograph albums, packs of cards, pots, necklaces, paste jewellery. To the left, an old oak wardrobe and two clothes horses of wood and brass would stand opposite a small wing-chair upholstered in thin-striped grey silk and a dressing table. Through a half-open door giving on to a bathroom you would glimpse thick bath-robes, swan-neck taps in solid brass, a large adjustable mirror, a pair of cut-throat razors and their green leather sheaths, bottles, horn-handled brushes, sponges. The bed-room walls would be papered with chintz; the bedspread would be a tartan blanket. A bedside table, with an open-work copper band running round three of its sides, would support a silver candlestick lamp topped with a very pale grey silk shade, a square carriage clock, a rose in a stem-vase, and, on its lower shelf, folded newspapers and some magazines. Further on, at the foot of the bed, there would be a big pouf in natural hide. At the window, the gauze curtains would slide on brass rods; the thick woollen double curtains would be half drawn. In the half-light the room would still be bright. On the wall, above the bed made up and turned down for the night, between two small wall lamps, the astonishing, long, narrow black-and-white photograph of a bird in the sky would surprise you by its slightly formal perfection.

The second door would reveal a study. From top to bottom the walls would be lined with books and periodicals with, here and there, so as to break the continuity of bindings and jackets, a number of prints, drawings and photographs – Antonello da Messina's *Saint Jerome*, a detail from *The Triumph of Saint George*, one of Piranesi's dungeons, a portrait by Ingres, a little pen-and-ink landscape by Klee, a sepia-tint photograph of Renan in his room at the Collège de France, a Steinberg department store, Cranach's *Melanchthon* – pinned to wooden panels set into the shelving. Slightly to the left of the window and at a shallow angle would be a long country table covered with a large red blotter. Wooden boxes, flat pen-holders and pots of all kinds would hold pencils, paper-clips, staples large and small. A glass tile would serve as an ashtray. A circular black leather box decorated with gold-leaf arabesques would be filled with cigarettes. Light would come from an old desk-lamp, adjustable only with difficulty, fitted with a green opaline lampshade shaped like a visor. On each side of the table, virtually facing each other, would be two high-backed wood and leather armchairs. Still further to the left, along the wall, would be a narrow table overflowing with books. A wing-chair in bottle-green leather would lead to grey metal filing cabinets and light wooden card-index boxes. On a third, even smaller table would be a Swedish lamp and a typewriter under its canvas dust-cover. Right at the back would be a narrow bed covered in ultramarine velvet and stacked with cushions of all colours. On a painted wooden stand, almost in the middle of the room, there would be a globe made of papier-mâché and nickel silver, illustrated in naïf style, a fake antique. Behind the desk, half-hidden by the red curtain at the window, would be an oiled-wood ladder which could slide on a brass rail all the way round the room.

There, life would be easy, simple. All the servitudes, all the problems brought by material existence would find a natural solution. A cleaning lady would come every morning. Every fortnight, wine, oil and sugar would be delivered. There would be a huge, bright kitchen with blue tiles decorated with heraldic emblems, three china plates decorated with yellow arabesques in metallic paint, cupboards everywhere, a handsome whitewood table in the middle with stools and bench-seats. It would be pleasant to come and sit there, every morning, after a shower, scarcely dressed. On the table there would be a sizeable stoneware butter dish, jars of marmalade, honey, toast, grapefruit cut in two. It would be early. It would be May, the start of a long summer's day.

They would open the mail, they would open the newspapers. They would light their first cigarette. They would go out. Their work would keep them busy for a few hours only, in the morning. They would meet for lunch, a sandwich or a steak, according to their mood; they would have coffee at a street café and then go home, on foot, slowly.

Their flat would rarely be tidy, but its very untidiness would be its greatest charm. They would hardly bother themselves with it: they would live in it. The comfort of their surroundings would seem to them to be an established fact, a datum, a state of their nature. Their attention would be elsewhere: on the book they would open, on the text they would draft, on the record they would listen to, on their dialogue engaged afresh each day. They would work for a long while. Then they would dine, or go out for dinner; they would see old friends; they would walk together.

Sometimes it would seem to them that a whole life could be led harmoniously between these book-lined walls, amongst these objects so perfectly domesticated that they would have ended up believing these bright, soft, simple and beautiful things had only ever been made for their sole use. But they wouldn't feel enslaved by them: on some days, they would go off on a chance adventure. No plan seemed impossible to them. They would not know rancour, or bitterness, or envy. For their means and their desires would always match in all ways. They would call this balance happiness and, with their freedom, with their wisdom and their culture, they would know how to retain and to reveal it in every moment of their living, together.

II

They would have liked to be rich. They believed they would have been up to it. They would have known how to dress, how to look and how to smile like rich people. They would have had the requisite tact and discretion. They would have forgotten they were rich, would have grasped how not to flaunt their wealth. They wouldn't have taken pride in it. They would have drunk it into themselves. Their pleasures would have been intense. They would have liked to wander, to dawdle, to choose, to savour. They would have liked to live. Their lives would have been an art of living.

But such things are far from easy. For this young couple, who were not rich but wanted to be, simply because they were not poor, there could be no situation more awkward. They had only what they deserved to have. They were thrown, when already they were dreaming of space, light, silence, back to the reality, which was not even miserable, but simply cramped (and that was perhaps even worse), of their tiny flat, of their everyday meals, of their puny holidays. That was what corresponded to their economic status, to their social situation. That was their reality and they had no other. But beside them, all around them, all along the streets where they could not but walk, existed the fallacious but nonetheless glowing offerings of antique-dealers, delicatessens and stationers. From Palais-Royal to Saint-Germain-des-Prés, from Champ-de-Mars to the Champs-Elysées, from the Luxembourg Gardens to

Montparnasse, from Ile Saint-Louis to the Marais, from Place des Ternes to Place de l'Opéra, from Madeleine to the Monceau Gardens, the whole of Paris was a perpetual temptation. They burned with desire to give in to it, passionately, straight away and for ever. But the horizon of their desires was mercilessly blocked; their great impossible dreams belonged only to utopia.

They lived in a quaint, low-ceilinged and tiny flat overlooking a garden. And as they remembered their garret – a gloomy, narrow, overheated corridor with clinging smells – they lived in their flat, to begin with, in a kind of intoxication, refreshed each morning by the sound of chirping birds. They would open the windows and, for many minutes, they would gaze, in utter happiness, at their courtyard. The building was old, not yet at all at the point of collapse, but dowdy and cracked. The corridors and staircases were narrow and dirty, dripping with damp, impregnated with greasy fumes. But in between two large trees and five tiny garden plots of irregular shapes, most of them overgrown but endowed with precious lawn, flowers in pots, bushes, even primitive statues, there wound a path made of rough, large paving stones which gave the whole thing a countryside air. It was one of those rare spots in Paris where it could happen, on some autumn days, after rain, that a smell would rise from the ground, an almost powerful smell of the forest, of earth, of rotting leaves.

They never tired of these charms and they always remained just as naturally responsive to them as they had been on the first day, but it became obvious, after a few care-free, jaunty months, that these attractions could in no way suffice to make them oblivious of the inadequacies of their dwelling. Accustomed to living in squalid rooms where all they did was to sleep, and to spending their days

28

in cafés, they took a long time to notice that the most banal functions of everyday life – sleeping, eating, reading, chatting, washing – each required a specific space, the manifest absence of which then began to make itself felt. They found consolation where they could, congratulated themselves on the excellent neighbourhood they were in, on the proximity of Rue Mouffetard and the Jardin des Plantes, on the quietness of the street, on the stylishness of their low ceilings, and on the magnificence of the trees and the courtyard through all the seasons; but indoors it all began to collapse under the heaps of objects, of furniture, books, plates, papers, empty bottles. A war of attrition began from which they would never emerge victorious.

With a total floor area of thirty-five square metres, which they never dared check, their flat consisted of a minute entrance hall, a cramped kitchen, half of which had been converted into a washroom, a modest-sized bedroom, an all-purpose room – library, living-room or study, spare bedroom – and an ill-defined nook, halfway between a broom-cupboard and a corridor, in which space had some-how been found for a matchbox fridge, an electric water-heater, an improvised wardrobe, a table, at which they ate, and a laundry-box which doubled up as a bench-seat.

On some days the lack of space became overwhelming. They would suffocate. But it was no use pushing back the boundaries of their two-roomed flatlet, no use knocking down walls, calling up corridors, cupboards, openings, no use imagining ideal wardrobes or taking over adjacent flats in their dreams, they would always end up back in what was their lot, their only lot: thirty-five square metres.

Judicious improvements would undoubtedly have been feasible: a partition wall could have been removed, freeing a huge and ill-used corner space, a too-bulky piece of furniture could be replaced advantageously, a set of cupboards could spring up. Doubtless, then, provided it was repainted, stripped, done up with a little love, their dwelling would have been unquestionably charming, with its one red-curtained window and its other window with green curtains, with its long, rather wobbly oak table that had been bought at the flea market filling the whole length of one wall section, beneath the very fine reproduction of a mariner's chart, and which a little roll-top Second Empire *escritoire* made of mahogany with inlaid brass beads, several missing, separated into two working desks – to the left, for Sylvie, to the right, for Jérôme – each signalled by an identical red blotter, an identical glass tile, an identical pencil-box; with its old pewter-rimmed glass jar that had been transformed into a lamp, with its metal-reinforced, wood-veneer seed-measuring jar which did as a waste-paper basket, with its two unmatched armchairs, its rush-seated chairs, its milking stool. And the neat, clean and ingenious whole would emanate friendliness and warmth, a wholesome aura of work and shared living.

But the mere prospect of the work involved scared them. They would have had to borrow, to save, to invest. They could not bring themselves to do it. Their hearts weren't in it: they thought only in terms of all or nothing. The bookcase would be light oak or it would not be. It was not. Books piled up on two dirty wooden shelving stacks, and, in double rows, in cupboards which should never have been used that way. For three years an electric point remained unrepaired, without their making up their minds to call in an electrician, whilst along almost every wall ran crudely spliced and shoddily extended leads. It took them six months to replace a curtain pulley-rope. And the slightest hold-up in regular maintenance resulted within twenty-four hours in a mess which the beneficent presence of trees and gardens so close at hand made even more unbearable.

The temporary, the provisional held absolute sway. They were in wait only of a miracle. They would have summoned architects, contractors, builders, plumbers, decorators and painters. They would have gone on a cruise and on their return would have found a flat transformed, converted, refurbished, a model apartment, miraculously enlarged, full of custom-built details, removable partitions, sliding doors, an efficient and unobtrusive heating system, invisible electrical wiring, good quality furniture.

But between these too grand daydreams in which they wallowed with strange self-indulgence, and their total lack of any actual doing, no rational plan, matching the objective necessities to their financial means, arose to fill the gap. The vastness of their desires paralysed them.

Such a lack of directness, of clear-headedness, almost, was typical. What was probably the most serious thing was that they were cruelly lacking in ease – not material, objective ease, but easiness, or a certain kind of relaxedness. They tended to be on edge, tense, avid, almost jealous. Their love of well-being, of higher living standards, came out most often as an idiotic kind of sermonising, when they would hold forth, they and their friends, on the sheer genius of a pipe or a low table; they would turn them into *objets d'art*, into museum pieces. They would become passionate about a suitcase – one of those tiny, astonishingly flat cases in slightly grainy black leather you could see on display in shop windows around Madeleine and which seem the quintessence of the alleged pleasures of lightning visits to New York or to London. They would cross all of Paris to see an armchair they'd been told was just perfect. And since they knew their classics they would sometimes even hesitate to put on some new garment, as it seemed so important to them, for it to look its best, that it should first have been worn three times. But the slightly ritualised gestures they would make to show their approval at a tailor's, or a milliner's, or a bootmaker's shop window display only managed, most often, to make them look slightly silly.

Perhaps they were too marked by their past (not they alone, moreover, but their friends, their colleagues, people of their age, the circles they mixed in). Perhaps they were too greedy from the outset: they wanted to go too fast. The world and its things would have had to have always belonged to them, and then they could have imprinted on them myriad signs of their ownership. But they were condemned to conquest; they could become richer and richer, but there was no way they could have always been rich. They would have liked to live in comfort, amidst beauty. But they shrieked, they admired, and that was the surest proof that they were not in it, not amidst it. They lacked tradition – in perhaps the most despicable sense of the word – as well as true enjoyment, implicit and immanent, like a self-evident truth, the enjoyment which involves bodily happiness; their pleasure was cerebral. Too often, what they liked in the things they called luxury was only the money behind them; they loved wealth before they loved life.

In this respect their first sallies outside the student world, their first forays into the universe of high-class shops which was soon to become their Promised Land, were particularly revealing. Their still-wavering taste, their over-hesitant meticulousness, their lack of experience, their rather blinkered respect for what they believed to be the standards of true good taste, brought them some jarring moments, some humiliations. For a time it might have appeared that the sartorial ideal to which Jérôme and his friends aspired was not that of the English gentleman, but the utterly continental caricature of it presented by a recent emigrant on a modest salary. And on the day Jérôme bought his first pair of British shoes, he took great care, after polishing them at length with a woollen rag dipped in a little beeswax of superior quality, rubbing very gently in small concentric circles, he took great care to put them in the sun where they were supposed to acquire an outstanding shine in the least time. Alas, alongside a pair of crepe-soled moccasin ankle-boots which he obstinately refused to wear, they were his only shoes; he misused them, dragged them through rutted tracks, and finished them off in just under seven months.

Then, as time passed, with the help of accumulating experience, it seemed that they were learning how to stand back a little from their most fervent passions. They had learned how to wait, and how to grow accustomed. Their taste matured slowly, became firmer, more balanced. Their desires had time to ripen; their greed became less sour. When on outings around Paris they stopped in villages to look at antiques, they no longer rushed straight towards the china plates, towards the church pews, towards the blown-glass demijohns and the brass candlesticks. To be sure, the somewhat static image they had of the ideal home, of perfect amenity, of the happy life was still imbued with a lot of naivety, a lot of self-indulgence: there was something forced in their liking for objects which only the taste of the day decreed to be beautiful: imitation Epinal pseudo-naive cartoons, English-style etchings, agates, spun-glass tumblers, neo-primitive paste jewellery, para-scientific apparatus, which in no time at all they would come across in all the window displays in Rue Jacob, in Rue Visconti. They still dreamt of possessing such things; they would have assuaged that obvious, instant need to be up-to-date, to be seen to be connoisseurs. But this extreme imitativeness was becoming less and less important, and it was pleasant for them to reflect that the picture they had of life had slowly been stripped of all its more aggressive, showy and occasionally juvenile trappings. They had burnt what they had previously worshipped: the witches' mirrors, the chopping-blocks, those stupid little mobiles, the radiometers, the multi-coloured pebbles, the hessian panels adorned with expressive squiggles as if by Mathieu. It seemed to them that they were progressively mastering their desires: they knew what they wanted; they had clear ideas. They knew what their happiness, their freedom would be.

But they were wrong all the same. They were beginning to lose their way. Already they were starting to feel they were being propelled along a path of which they knew neither the turns nor the terminus. They did on occasions feel frightened. Most often, however, all they felt was impatience: they felt ready; they were available; they were waiting to live, they were waiting for money.

III

Jérôme was twenty-four and Sylvie twenty-two. They were both market researchers. Their work, which was not exactly a trade nor quite a profession, consisted of interviewing people by various different techniques, on a range of subjects. It was difficult work, requiring at the very least a high degree of nervous concentration, but it was not uninteresting, not at all badly paid, and it left them an appreciable amount of free time.

Like almost all their colleagues, Jérôme and Sylvie had become market researchers by necessity and not by choice. No-one knows, in any case, where the untrammelled development of their natural inclinations towards idleness would have led them. There again, history had chosen for them. Of course, like everyone else, they would have liked to give themselves to something, to feel in themselves some powerful need that they would have called a vocation, an ambition that would have raised them up, a passion that would have fulfilled them. But they possessed, alas, but a single passion, the passion for a higher standard of living, and it exhausted them. When they were students the prospect of a mediocre degree and then a teaching post with a tiny salary at Nogent-sur-Seine, Château-Thierry or Etampes terrified them so much that virtually on meeting each other – Jérôme was then twenty one, Sylvie nineteen – and without needing to talk it over, they dropped out of courses they had never really begun. The thirst for knowledge did not torture them. Far more prosaically, and without hiding from the fact that they were probably making a mistake and that sooner or later they would come to regret it, they thirsted for a slightly bigger room, for running hot and cold water, for a shower, for meals more varied, or just more copious, than those they ate in student canteens, maybe for a car, for records, holidays, clothes.

Motivation research had emerged in France several years earlier. That year it was still expanding fast. New agencies were springing up by the month, out of nothing, or almost. You could get work in them easily. Most often it involved going into parks or standing at school gates or knocking on doors in suburban housing estates to ask housewives if they had noticed some recent advertisement and what they thought of it. These instant surveys, called minitests or quickies, earned a hundred francs each. It wasn't much, but it was better than baby-sitting, working as a night watchman or as a dishwasher, better than any of the other menial jobs – distributing leaflets, book-keeping, timing radio advertisements, hawking, cramming – which were traditionally the preserve of students. And then the very youth of the agencies themselves, their almost informal state of development, the still total absence of trained staff, held out the prospect, at least potentially, of rapid promotion and a dizzying rise in status.

It was not a bad guess. They spent a few months handing out survey questionnaires. Then came an agency director who, for lack of time, took a chance on them: and so they set off for the provinces with tape-recorders under their arms. Some of their fellow travellers, scarcely older than they were, introduced them to the techniques of the open and the closed interview, which were actually less difficult than is commonly supposed. They learned how to make other people do the talking and to weigh their own words carefully; they learned how to unearth from people's muddled hesitations, perplexed silences and shy hints the lines that needed pursuing; they pierced the secret of that universal "aha . . .", a truly magical intonation with which the interviewer punctuates the interviewee's words, to bolster his confidence, to show that he understands, to egg him on, to query and even sometimes to threaten him.

They obtained respectable results. They built on their success. They picked up, from here and from there, snippets of sociology, psychology, statistics; they acquired the vocabulary and the signs, the mannerisms that make the right impression: for Sylvie, a particular way of putting on and taking off her glasses, a particular way of taking notes, of thumbing through a report, a particular way of speaking, of inserting in her conversations with employers and in a barely interrogative tone of voice turns of phrase like "indeed . . .", "I guess maybe . . .", "up to a point . . .", "what I'm wondering is . . .", a particular way of quoting at appropriate points the names of C. Wright Mills, William Whyte, or – even better – Lazarsfeld, Cantril or Herbert Hyman, of whose works they had read not three pages.

They proved very adept at acquiring these indispensable basic items of professional equipment, and, scarcely one year after their first involvement in motivation research, they were entrusted with the highly responsible task of a "content analysis": it was one rung only below the role of project supervisor, which was always performed by an office-based executive, the highest, thus the best-paid and consequently the most prestigious position in the whole hierarchy. Over the following years they almost never slipped from these heights.

And so for four years and maybe more they explored and interviewed and analysed. Why are pure-suction vacuum cleaners selling so poorly? What do people of modest origin think of chicory? Do you like ready-made mashed potato, and if so, why? Because it's light? Because it's creamy? Because it's easy to make – just open it up and there you are? Do people really reckon baby carriages are expensive? Aren't you always prepared to fork out a bit extra for the good of the kids? Which way will French women vote? Do people like cheese in squeezy tubes? Are you for or against public transport? What do you notice first when you eat yoghurt? – the colour? the texture? the taste? natural odour? Do you read a lot, a little, not at all? Do you eat out? Would you, Madam, like to rent your room to a Black? What do people think, honestly, of old age pensions? What does the younger generation think? What do executives think? What does the woman of thirty think? What do you think of holidays? Where do you spend your holidays? Do you like frozen food? How much do you think a lighter like this one costs, eh? What do you look for in a mattress? Describe a man who likes pasta. What do you think of your washing machine? Are you satisfied with it? Doesn't it make too many suds? Does it wash properly? Does it tear the clothes? Does it dry? Would you rather have a washing machine that dries as well? And safety in coal mines, is it alright or not good enough, in your view, sir? (Make the target speak; ask him to give personal examples: things he has seen; has he been injured himself? How did it happen? And your son, sir, will he be a miner like his father? So what will he be, then?)

There was washing, drying, ironing. Gas, electricity and the telephone. Children. Clothes and underclothes. Mustard. Packet soups, tinned soups. Hair: how to wash it, how to dry it, how to make it hold a wave, how to make it shine. Students, fingernails, cough syrup, typewriters, fertilisers, tractors, leisure pursuits, presents, stationery, linen, politics, motorways, alcoholic drinks, mineral water, cheeses, jams, lamps and curtains, insurance and gardening. *Nil humani alienum* . . . Nothing that was human was outside their scope.

For the first time they earned some money. They did not like their work; could they have liked it? But they did not dislike it a great deal either. They felt they were learning a lot from it. Year after year it changed them completely.

These were their great days of conquest. They had nothing; they were discovering the riches of the world.

For years they had been absolutely anonymous. They dressed like students, that is to say badly. Sylvie had a single skirt, ugly jumpers, a pair of cord trousers, a duffle-coat; Jérôme had a mucky parka, an off-the-peg suit, one pitiful necktie. They leapt ecstatically into fashionable English clothes. They discovered knitwear, silk blouses, shirts by Doucet, cotton voile ties, silk scarves, tweed, lambswool, cashmere, vicuna, leather and jerseywool, flax and, finally, the great staircase of footwear leading from Churches to Westons, from Westons to Buntings and from Buntings to Lobbs.

Their dream was a trip to London. They would have split their time between the National Gallery, Savile Row and a particular pub in Church Street which had stuck with feeling in Jérôme's memory. But they were not yet rich enough to kit themselves out from top to toe in London. In Paris, the first money gaily earned by the sweat of their brows, Sylvie spent on shopping: a knitted silk bodice from Cornuel, an imported lambswool twinset, a straight, formal skirt, extremely soft plaited leather shoes, and a big silk headscarf with a peacock-and-foliage pattern. Jérôme, for his part, though he was still fond of shuffling around from time to time in clogs, unshaven, wearing an old collarless shirt and denim trousers, went in for total contrasts and discovered the joys of lazy mornings: taking a bath, shaving very close, sprinkling *eau-de-toilette*, slipping on over still damp skin a shirt of unimpeachable whiteness, tying a woollen or silken necktie. He bought three of these, at Old England, together with a tweed jacket, some marked-down shirts and a pair of shoes he thought he would not be embarrassed to wear.

Then – and this was one of the important days of their lives – they came across the Flea Market. Splendid, long-collared, button-down Arrow and Van Heusen shirts, at that time unfindable in Paris shops but which American comedy films were making increasingly popular (at least for that marginal set of people who delight in American comedies) were to be found there in untidy heaps, alongside allegedly indestructible trench coats, skirts, blouses, silk dresses, hide jackets and soft leather moccasins. They went every fortnight, on Saturday mornings, for a year or more, to rummage through tea-chests, display stalls, stacks, boxes, upturned umbrellas, amongst crowds of teenagers with long sideburns, Algerian watch-pedlars and American tourists who emerged from the glass eyes, shiny top hats and hobby-horses of the Vernaison market and wandered in a state of mild bewilderment around the Malik market, pondering on the strange fate of things, laid out alongside used nails, second-hand mattresses, machines of which only the casing remained, and spare parts, things which were but the slightly imperfect surplus stock of America's most celebrated shirtmakers. And they would bring back all kinds of clothes wrapped in newspaper, trinkets, umbrellas, old pots, satchels, records.

They were changing, becoming other people. It wasn't so much because of their (nonetheless genuine) need to differentiate themselves from the people it was their job to interview, to impress without overwhelming them. Nor was it because they met a lot of people, because they were taking their leave, for ever, or so they thought, from what had been their milieu. But money – and this point cannot but be an obvious one – creates new needs. They would have been surprised to realise, if they had thought about it for a moment – but in those years they didn't think – to what extent their views of their own bodies had altered, and, beyond that, their vision of everything that affected them, of everything that mattered, of everything that was in the process of becoming their world.

Everything was new. Their sensibilities, their tastes and their position propelled them towards things they had never known. They paid attention to the way others dressed; they noticed the furniture, the knick-knacks and the ties displayed in shop windows; they mused on estate agents' advertisements. They felt as if they understood things they had never bothered about before: it had come to matter to them whether a neighbourhood or a street was sad or jolly, quiet or noisy, deserted or lively. Nothing, ever, had equipped them for such new concerns. They discovered them enthusiastically, with a kind of freshness, and were bemused by having spent so long in ignorance. They felt no surprise, or almost none, at the fact that they thought about almost nothing else.

The paths they were following, the values they were gradually adopting, their outlook, their desires and their ambitions, it must be said, did indeed sometimes all feel desperately empty. They knew nothing that was not precarious or puzzling. Yet this was their life, it was the source of unsuspected experiences elating beyond intoxication, it was something hugely, intensely open. Sometimes they thought that the lives they would lead would be as magical, as flexible, as whimsical as American comedy films or title sequences by Saul Bass; and miraculous, luminous visions of pristine snow-covered fields crossed by lines of ski-tracks, of blue seas, sun, verdant hills, of logs crackling in stone hearths, of spectacular motorways, of pullmans and palatial hotels caressed them, as if they were promises.

They gave up their room and student canteens. Just next to the Jardin des Plantes, opposite the Paris Mosque, at 7, Rue de Quatrefages, they found a little two-roomed flat to rent, giving on to a pretty courtyard garden. They wanted carpets, tables, armchairs, sofas.

Those were the years when they wandered endlessly around Paris. They would stop at every antique dealer's. They would go in to department stores and stay for hours on end, marvelling and already scared but not daring to admit it to themselves, not daring to face squarely that particular type of despicable voracity which was to become their fate, their *raison d'être*, their watchword, for they were still marvelling at and almost drowning under the scale of their own needs, of the riches laid out before them, of the abundance on offer.

They discovered the smart little restaurants near Gobelins, Ternes, Saint-Sulpice, the empty bars where, on weekend trips away from Paris you can enjoy whispering, long walks in the woods, in autumn, at Rambouillet, Vaux and Compiègne, the almost perfect pleasure proffered in every place to the ear, to the eye and to the palate.

And so, step by step, as they took their place in the real world in a rather deeper way than in the past when, as the children of middle-class families of no substance and then as undifferentiated students without individual form, they had had but a superficial and skimpy view of the world, that is how they began to grasp what it meant to be a person of standing.

This concluding revelation, which, strictly speaking, was not a revelation at all but the culmination of the long-drawn-out process of their social and psychological maturing, and of which they would not have been able to describe the steps without a great deal of difficulty, put the final touch on their metamorphosis.

IV

Life, for them, and their circle of friends, was often a whirlwind.

There was a whole crowd of them, they made a fine bunch. They knew each other well; taking a lot from each other, they had common habits, common tastes and shared memories. They had their own vocabulary, their own marks, their special ideas. Too sophisticated to be perfectly similar to each other, but probably not sophisticated enough to avoid imitating each other more or less consciously, they spent a large part of their lives swapping things. They felt irritated by that often enough; but even more often they found it amusing.

Almost all of them belonged to advertising circles. Some, however, were still pursuing, or trying to pursue, some kind of degree course or other. Most often they had met in the flashy or pseudo-functional setting of an agency boss's office. They would listen side by side, aggressively pencilling on their blotters their petty suggestions and their grisly jokes; their shared contempt for those fat cats, those profiteers, for those eye-wash merchants, was sometimes their first meeting ground. But most often they felt at first as if they had been sentenced to spending five or six days together in dreary small-town hotels. At each meal taken they would invite friendship to share their table. But lunches were hasty and business-like, dinners dreadfully slow, unless something ignited that miraculous spark which would brighten their mournful, travelling salesmen's faces, make this evening in the provinces a memorable occasion, and turn a very ordinary pâté put on the bill as an extra by some crooked hotelier into a succulent treat. Only then could they forget their tape-recorders, abandon the over-guarded tones of senior psychologists. They would linger at the dinner table. They would talk about themselves and about things in general, about nothing in particular, about their tastes and their ambitions. They would scour the town to find the one really comfortable bar it simply had to have, and, until a very late hour, in front of whiskies, brandies, gins and tonic, they would conjure up, with an almost ritualised carefree abandon, the stories of their love-affairs, their desires, their travels, the things they wouldn't do, the things they adored passionately, without being surprised about – on the contrary, being almost delighted by – the likeness of their different histories, the sameness of their points of view.

Sometimes these nascent sympathies gave birth only to distant acquaintance, telephone calls at lengthening intervals. Sometimes, too, though rather less often in fact, whether by chance or by mutual desire, they set in train, slowly or less slowly, a potential friendship which would develop in stages. In that way, over the years, they had slowly knit together.

They were, all of them, easily identifiable. They had money, not too much, but enough to fall only intermittently – because of some crazy purchase, perhaps superfluous, perhaps necessary, they really wouldn't have been able to say which – into genuine debt. Their flats, flatlets, lofts, two-roomed conversions in dilapidated houses, in selected neighbourhoods – Palais-Royal, Contrescarpe, Saint-Germain, Luxembourg, Montparnasse – were very similar: the same dirt-encrusted sofas, the same allegedly rustic tables, the same heaps of books and records, old glassware and old jars used, indiscriminately, for flowers, pencils, small change, cigarettes, sweets and paper-clips. They dressed roughly in the same fashion, that is to say with that middling tastefulness which, for men as for women, is what is so right about *Madame Express* and, by repercussion, about her husband also. What is more, they owed a great deal to that ideal couple in the women's pages of their favourite weekly magazine.

L'Express was without doubt the one weekly magazine to which they paid heed. They didn't actually like it very much, but they bought it or, at the least, borrowed it from each other, read it regularly and often, they confessed, even kept back-numbers. As a matter of fact, they disagreed very frequently with the political line taken by *L'Express* (on one occasion, they had penned in righteous indignation a slim pamphlet against "The Style of the Lieutenant-Editor") and for news analysis they preferred *Le Monde* by far, which they subscribed to faithfully to a man, or even the positions adopted by *Libération*, which they tended to consider a decent sort of newspaper. But *L'Express*, and that magazine alone, matched their art of living; each week, they would find in its pages – and it did not matter whether they could view them justifiably as misrepresented or distorted – the really current issues in their daily lives. Not infrequently they took offence. For in all honesty the style, heavily marked by false modesty, the implied meanings, the veiled contempt, the ill-digested envy, the shallow crazes, the kicks in the shins, the knowing winks, together with the great advertising parade which made up *L'Express* in its entirety – its end and not its means, its most necessary aspect – as well as those little details which mean everything, those bargain items which were supposed to be really fun, those businessmen who understood the real issues, those specialists who knew what they were talking about and made sure you knew it too, those bold thinkers, pipe-suckers all, who were dragging the world into the twentieth century; in short, that panel of responsible directors who foregathered each week around a table or in a forum and whose po-faced smiles made you think they were still clasping in their right hands the golden key to the managers' toilets – all that could not fail to make them think (as they repeated the not very good pun with which their pamphlet had begun) that though it was not obvious that *L'Express* was a *left-wing paper*, it was as clear as daylight that it was a *sinister* one. That wasn't right either, as they well knew, but it reassured them.

They didn't hide from the fact that they were made for *L'Express*. No doubt they needed their freedom, their intelligence, their high spirits and their youth to be, at all times and in all places, properly represented. They allowed *L'Express* to take them under its wing, because it was the simplest thing to do, because their contempt for it kept their consciences clear. And the harshness of their judgment was equalled only by the extent of their submission to it: they thumbed through the magazine muttering curses, they would crumple it up and throw it away. They would go on for hours, sometimes, in high dudgeon at its outrageousness. But they read it, indisputably, and they took it all in.

Where could they have found a truer image of their tastes and yearnings? Were they not young? Were they not wealthy, up to a point? *L'Express* held out to them all the signs of comfortable living: thick bathrobes, brilliant unravellings of murky truths, fashionable beaches, exotic cookery, useful tips, intelligent news analysis, the secrets of the gods, places out in the sticks where you could pick up property for almost nothing, the names of the different carillon bells, new ideas, smart outfits, frozen food, elegant accessories, the scandals of polite society, up-to-the-minute advice.

They would dream, half aloud, of chesterfield settees.

L'Express would dream with them. They would spend a large part of their holidays doing the country-house auctions; there, at bargain prices, they acquired pewter, straw-bottomed chairs, glasses that asked to be drunk from, horn-handled knives, shiny bowls which they made into precious ashtrays. All these things, they knew, had been, or would be mentioned in the *L'Express*.

Their actual purchasing practice, however, was quite significantly different from the shopping habits put forward by *L'Express*. They were not yet quite "settled down" and, although their "executive" status was broadly acknowledged, they did not enjoy the job security or the bonus payments or the salary enhancements of permanent staff under contract. *L'Express* suggested, in that case, by way of pleasant but inexpensive boutiques (the boss is a pal, he'll give you a drink and an open sandwich whilst you're making up your mind), little businesses where fashion had required, in order to create an appropriate impression, a thoroughgoing improvement of all previous fixtures and fittings: whitewashed walls were indispensable, dark brown carpeting a necessity, which could be replaced only by a mosaic of antiquated floor tiles of different kinds; exposed beams were obligatory, and little internal staircases, real fireplaces with a fire burning, rustic or (even better) Provençal furniture were highly recommended. These conversions which were spreading across Paris and affecting, indiscriminately, bookshops, art galleries, haberdashers', novelty and furniture stores, and even grocers' shops (it was not uncommon to see some formerly down-at-heel corner-shop grocer turn into a Cheese Consultant complete with a blue apron giving him a very expert air, and his shop acquire roof-beams and straw decking . . .), such conversions, therefore, brought more or less legitimately in their wake a rise in prices such that the purchase of a raw-wool, hand-printed dress, of a cashmere twinset woven by a blind Orkney crofter (*exclusive genuine vegetable-dyed hand-spun hand-woven*) or of a sumptuous jerseywool and leather jacket (for weekend wear, for hunting, for driving) proved permanently impossible. They would eye the wares of antique-dealers closely, but to furnish their flat they actually relied on country sales or the less-publicised auctions at Drouot (and even there they went less often than they would have liked); similarly, all of them only enlarged their stock of clothes by assiduous excursions to the Flea Market or, twice a year, to jumble sales organised by English ladies in aid of the Saint George's English Church's charitable works, where there were plenty of diplomats' cast-offs, in perfectly acceptable condition of course. Often they felt awkward about it: they would have to push their way through a milling crowd and rummage through piles of ghastly stuff – the taste of the English is not all it's cracked up to be – before unearthing a splendid tie, no doubt too frivolous for an Embassy under-secretary, or a shirt that had once been exquisite, or a skirt that would just need taking up. But, of course, it was that or nothing: the incommensurability, perceptible in every domain, between the quality of their taste in clothing (nothing was too fine for them) and the amount of money they normally had available was an obvious, if ultimately secondary, sign of their material situation. They were not the only ones; rather than shop at the sales, which happened everywhere, three times a year, they preferred to buy second-hand. In the world that was theirs it was almost a regulation always to wish for more than you could have. It was not they who had decreed it; it was a social law, a fact of life, which advertising in general, magazines, window displays, the street scene and even, in a certain sense, all those productions which in common parlance constitute cultural life, expressed most authentically. That was why they were wrong to feel, on

49

some occasions, that they were losing their dignity. For minor mortifications – having to ask the price of something, hesitantly; having to think twice; trying to haggle; window-shopping, not daring to go in; wanting; appearing mean and petty – are also what keep business going. They were proud of having got something cheap, of having spent nothing on it, hardly a penny. They were even prouder (but the pleasure of paying too much for something has its own price, which is always a bit too high) to have paid a great deal, the highest possible price, on an impulse, without questioning, almost in blind excitement, for something that could not fail to be the finest, uniquely fine, perfect. These moments of shame and pride both had the same function, brought identical disappointments, identical inner rages. And they grasped – since all around them, everywhere, everything made them grasp, since slogans, posters, neon-lit signs and floodlit shop windows drummed it into their heads from morning to night – that they were for ever one rung down on the ladder, always one rung too low; even though they were fortunate enough not to be, not by a long chalk, at the bottom of the pile.

They were the "new generation", young executives who had not yet cut all their teeth, technocrats on the way, but only halfway, to success. Almost all of them came from the lower middle classes, whose values, they felt, were for them no longer adequate. They cast their eyes enviously, desperately, towards the visible comfort, luxury and perfection of the upper middle classes. They had no past, no tradition. There were no inheritances to wait for. Of all of Jérôme's and Sylvie's friends, only one came from a wealthy, well-established family: they were textile wholesalers in Lille, with a comfortable pile conveniently invested in property in Lille, in a portfolio, a country house near Beauvais, gold and silver plate, jewellery, and roomfuls of antique furniture. All the others had spent their childhoods in dining rooms and bedrooms with imitation Chippendale or imitation rustic furniture as such things were imagined initially at the dawn of the 1930s – full-size beds covered with puce taffeta, three-door wardrobes with mirrors and gilded mouldings, horribly square tables on turned-wood legs, imitation antler coat-stands. In such surroundings, in the evening, beneath the family lamp, they had done their homework. They had taken down the rubbish, they had gone "off with the pail" to fetch the milk, they had slammed doors behind them. Their memories of childhood were all similar, just as the paths they had followed, their slow departures from their family backgrounds, and the vistas they thought they had chosen for themselves, were identical.

They were therefore of their own time. They were at ease with themselves. They were not, so they said, completely fooled. They could keep their distance. They were relaxed, or at least they tried to be. They had a sense of humour. They were by no means dim.

A detailed analysis would have detected easily enough, within the group they constituted, divergent trends, stifled enmities. Any sociometrist with an eye for finicky detail would have easily discovered in their midst fault lines, reciprocal exclusions, latent hostilities amongst them. It sometimes happened that one or another of them, in response to some more or less fortuitous accident, or a camouflaged provocation, or a misunderstanding all in hints, would spread discord amongst them. Their fine friendship would then disintegrate. They would then realise, with simulated amazement, that X, whom they'd always thought a generous chap, was the very soul of stinginess, that Y was nothing but a desiccated egoist.

Strains followed, and matured into break-ups. Sometimes they took malicious pleasure in setting one group up against another. Or alternatively there were protracted periods of sulking, of pronounced distance, of coldness. They would avoid each other and continually find ways of justifying their avoidance, until the hour of forgiving, forgetting and of reconciliation came round. For in the last analysis they could not manage without each other.

They played these games intensely and they spent on them precious time which they could have used without disadvantage to quite different ends. But they were such that, even if it occasionally irritated them, the group they constituted defined them almost entirely. Outside of it they had no real life. They were wise enough, none the less, not to see each other too often, not to work together always, and they even made an effort to keep up individual pursuits, private spheres to which they could withdraw, where they could forget, up to a point, not the group itself, the mafia, the team, but, obviously, the work on which it was based. Their almost shared lives made it easier to launch surveys, to go on trips to the provinces, to spend nights on analyses or on drafting reports; but it also tied them down to working like that. That, to tell the truth, was their awkward secret, their common weak spot. That was what they never mentioned.

Their greatest pleasure was to forget together, that is to say to indulge in distractions. They loved drinking, in the first place, and they drank a lot, often, together. They were habitués of "Harry's New York Bar", denizens of Rue Daunou, frequenters of the cafés in the Palais-Royal arcades, of "Le Balzar", of "Lipp", and a few other bars. They liked Munich beer, Guinness, gin, hot or cold punch, fruit liqueurs. Sometimes they spent whole evenings just drinking, huddled round two tables put together for the purpose, and they would talk, interminably, about the life they would have liked to lead, about the books they would write one day, about the things they would like to do, about the films they had seen or were going to see, the future of humanity, the political situation, their next holiday, their last holiday, an outing to the country, a short trip to Bruges, Antwerp or Basel. And on occasions, as they plunged ever deeper into these collective daydreams, not seeking to wake from them but continually refuelling them in unstated collusion, they would, eventually, lose all touch with reality. On such occasions, now and again a hand would simply emerge from the conclave: the waiter was there, to clear the empty tankards and bring full ones; and then their conversation, as it once again thickened, would consist solely of matter related to what they had just drunk, to their drunkenness, their thirst, their happiness.

They were in love with liberty. It seemed to them that the whole world was tailor-made for them. They lived at the exact tempo of their thirst, and their exuberance was irrepressible; their enthusiasm knew no bounds. They could have walked, run, danced, sung all night.

They wouldn't meet the day after. The couples would stay at home, dieting, feeling queasy, overindulging in black coffee and soluble aspirin. They would venture out only once night had fallen, to go and eat a plain steak in an expensive café. They would make draconian resolutions: no more smoking, no more drinking, no more wasting money. They would feel empty and stupid, and in their memory of their magnificent drinking bout there would always be a hint of yearning, a vague annoyance, a feeling of ambiguity, as if the very impulse which had made them drink had only reawakened in them a much deeper perplexity, a more hermetic contradiction from which they could not abstract themselves.

*

53

Or else, in the flat of one or another of them, they would hold almost monstrous dinner parties, veritable feasts. For the most part they had only tiny and sometimes unusable kitchens, and mixed sets of crockery with an odd few rather high-class pieces amongst them. Extremely delicate cut glass stood on the table beside recycled mustard jars, kitchen knives lay alongside little silver spoons with coats of arms.

They would return all together from Rue Mouffetard, arms laden with edibles, with whole trays of melons and peaches, and baskets filled with cheeses, legs of lamb, poultry, and paniers of oysters in season, and dishes of pâté, and fish roes, and, of course, with bottles, whole stacks of bottles of wine, port, mineral water, Coca-Cola.

Nine or ten people filled the narrow room, which was lit by a single window looking out on to the courtyard. A settee upholstered in coarse brown velvet occupied a recess at the far end; three would be placed there, the table set in front of them, and the others would sit on unmatched chairs and on stools. They would eat and drink for hours on end. The exuberance and the copiousness of these meals were odd: to be honest, and from a strictly culinary point of view, they were rather poor meals: roast meat and poultry without any sauce; the vegetables were almost invariably boiled or sauté potatoes or even, on days before pay-day, the main dish might be just pasta or rice garnished with olives and some anchovies. They didn't experiment at all; their most complicated dishes were melon in port, bananas *flambé*, cucumber salad in cream. It took them several years to realise that there was a technique, if not an art, of cookery, and that everything that they had enjoyed eating had been plain fare, unadorned, devoid of subtlety.

In that respect they demonstrated the ambiguity of their situation in life. What they took to be a feast corresponded in every particular to the only kind of meals they had known for years, namely student canteen food. By dint of eating tough and wafer-thin steaks, they had taken to worshipping Chateaubriand and fillet steaks. Meat in gravy – for years they looked askance at braised meat – did not attract them; they had too clear a memory of lumps of fat swimming around three slices of carrot in close proximity to a soggy piece of soft cheese and a spoonful of gelatinous jam. In a way, they liked anything which made a show without showing it had been cooked. They liked the visible signs of abundance and riches; they would have no truck with the slow process of elaboration which turns difficult raw materials into dishes, and which implies a whole world of pans, pots, slicers, strainers and ovens. But the sight of salami sometimes almost made them faint, because it was all immediately and entirely edible. They liked pâtés and ready-made diced vegetable salads decorated with mayonnaise whorls, boned ham and eggs in aspic: they yielded too often to such temptations, and regretted it, once their eyes had had their fill, almost as soon as they plunged their forks into the jelly enhanced by a slice of tomato and two sprigs of parsley. After all, it was only a hard-boiled egg.

Above all, they had the cinema. And this was probably the only area where they had learned everything from their own sensibilities. They owed nothing to models. Their age and education made them members of that first generation for which the cinema was not so much an art as simply a given fact; they had always known the cinema not as a fledgling art form but, from their earliest acquaintance, as a domain having its own masterworks and its own mythology. Sometimes it seemed as if they had grown up with it, and that they understood it better than anyone before them had ever been able to understand it.

They were cinema buffs. Film was their primordial passion; they indulged it every evening, or nearly. They loved the pictures as long as they were beautiful, entrancing, charming, fascinating. They loved the mastery of space, time and movement, they loved the whirl of New York streets, the torpor of the Tropics, fights in saloon bars. They were not excessively sectarian, like those dull minds which swear only by a single Eisenstein, Buñuel or Antonioni, or even – as there's no accounting for tastes – by Carné, Vidor, Aldrich or Hitchcock; nor were they too eclectic, like those infantile people who throw all critical sense to the winds and acclaim a director as a genius if he makes a blue sky look blue or if the pale red of Cyd Charisse's dress is made to clash with the darker red of Robert Taylor's sofa. They did not lack taste. They were highly suspicious of so-called art movies, with the result that when this term was not enough to spoil a film for them, they would find it even more beautiful (but they would say – quite rightly – that *Marienbad* was "all the same just a load of crap!"); they had an almost exaggerated feeling for Westerns, for thrillers, for American comedies and for those astonishing adventures full of lyrical flights, sumptuous images and dazzling, almost inexplicable beauties such as (the titles were imprinted on their minds for ever) *Lola, Bhowani Junction, The Bad and the Beautiful, Written on the Wind*.

They did not go to concerts at all often, and even less often to the theatre. But they would meet, by chance, at the Film Theatre, at the Passy Cinema, or the Napoleon, or in little local flea-pits – the Kursaal at Gobelins, the Texas at Montparnasse, the Bikini, the Mexico at Place Clichy, the Alcazar at Belleville, and others besides, around Bastille or in the XVth *arrondissement*, graceless, ill-equipped cinemas frequented by the unemployed, Algerians, ageing bachelors, and film buffs, where they would see, in atrociously dubbed French versions, those unknown masterpieces they remembered from when they were fifteen, or those reputed works of genius (they had memorised the entire list) which they had been trying in vain for years to see. They would always remember with wonderment the blessed evening when they had discovered, or rediscovered, almost by chance, *The Crimson Pirate*, *The World in His Arms*, *Night and the City*, *My Sister Eileen*, or *The Five Thousand Fingers of Dr T*. Alas, quite often, to tell the truth, they were horribly let down. Films they had waited so long for, as they had thumbed almost feverishly through the new issues of the *Entertainment Guide* every Wednesday, films they had been told by almost everyone were magnificent, sometimes did finally turn out to be showing somewhere. They would turn up, every one of them, on the opening night. The screen would light up, they would feel a thrill of satisfaction. But the colours had faded with age, the picture wobbled on the screen, the women were of another age; they would come out; they would be sad. It was not the film they had dreamt of. It was not the total film each of them had inside himself, the perfect film they could have enjoyed for ever and ever. The film they would have liked to make. Or, more secretly, no doubt, the film they would have liked to live.

V

So that was their life, as they lived it, as their friends lived,
in cluttered and charming flats, with their outings and
their films, their grand comradely dinner parties and their
wondrous plans. They were not unhappy. Fleeting, surrep-
titious moments of bliss in living lit up their days. Some
evenings, after dinner, they would linger at table, to finish
off a bottle of wine, nibble some nuts, light cigarettes.
Some nights they wouldn't manage to get to sleep and,
half sitting up, propped up by pillows, an ashtray shared
between them, they would talk until dawn. Some days
they would walk and talk for hours on end. They would
smile at each other's reflections in shop windows. It
would seem to them that everything was perfect. They
would walk unconstrainedly, with loose limbs, untouched,
it seemed, by the passing of time. Simply being there, in
the street, on a crisp, cold, blustery day, wrapped in warm
clothing, at dusk, proceeding smartly but unhurriedly
towards a place of friendship, was enough to make their
smallest gestures – lighting a cigarette, buying a bag of hot
chestnuts, negotiating a way through the crowd at a station
exit – appear to them as the direct and obvious expression
of a boundless bliss.

Or again, on some summer nights they would walk for
miles through neighbourhoods they did not know. The
moon's round orb would shine high in the sky, casting its
velvety light on every thing. The long, wide, empty streets
would reverberate with the sound of their footsteps, as

they walked all in step. Taxis would go by seldom, slowly, almost noiselessly. On such nights they had the world in their arms. It was unimaginably exhilarating, as if they had been entrusted with fabulous secrets and inexpressible powers. And they would hold hands and begin to run, or to play hopscotch, or to run a hopping race along the pavement, whilst bellowing in unison the great arias of *Così fan tutte* or the *B Minor Mass*.

Or again, they would push open a door into a small restaurant and joyfully, almost ritually, absorb the ambient warmth, the clutter of cutlery, the clinking of glasses, the muffled sounds of conversation, the inviting whiteness of napkins. They would select their wine punctiliously, unfold their napkins, and then it would seem to them, as they sat in the warm, in a close huddle, smoking a cigarette to be stubbed out in a moment's time when the hors d'oeuvres would arrive, that their life was going to be only the infinite sum of such auspicious moments, and that they would always be happy, because they deserved to be happy, because they would manage to stay free, because happiness was within them. They would sit facing each other, they were going to eat after having been hungry, and all these things – the thick white tablecloth, the blue blot of a packet of *Gitanes*, the earthenware plates, the rather heavy cutlery, the stem glasses, the wicker basket full of newly baked bread – constituted the ever-fresh setting of an almost visceral pleasure, a pleasure so intense as to verge on numbness: an impression, almost exactly opposite and almost exactly identical to the experience of speed, of a tremendous stability, of tremendous plenitude. From this table set for dinner arose for them the feeling of perfect synchrony: they were in tune with the world, they were swimming in it, in their element, with nothing to fear from it.

Perhaps they were a bit more adept than others at making out or even provoking these auguries of good fortune.

Their ears, their fingers, their palates – permanently on the alert, as it were – lay in wait only for such propitious instants, which could be set off by minute details. But when they surrendered to those feelings of unruffled beatitude, of eternity undisturbed by the slightest ripple, when everything was in balance, deliciously slow, the very intensity of their bliss underlined the ephemerality and fragility of such instants. It did not take much to make it all crumble: the slightest false note, a mere moment's hesitation, a sign that was perhaps too vulgar, and their happiness would be put out of joint; it went back to being what it always had been, a kind of deal, a thing they had bought, a pitiful and flimsy thing, just a second's respite which returned them all the more forcefully to the real dangers, the real uncertainties in their lives, in their history.

The trouble with market researching is that it can't go on for ever. The day was already marked down in Jérôme's and Sylvie's history when they would have to choose between unemployment, or underemployment, on the one side, or, on the other, a fuller kind of involvement in an agency – a full-time job, with executive status. Or else change their careers, find a job in some other line; but that would have only shifted the same problem to another terrain. For if it is commonly accepted that people who have not yet reached thirty may remain relatively independent and work as and when it suits them, even if their availability, openness of mind, the variety of their experience and what is still called their adaptability is sometimes valued, it is on the other hand required, paradoxically, of any potential partner, once he has passed the milestone of his thirtieth birthday (and this is, precisely, what makes your thirtieth birthday a milestone) that he show some evidence of stability, provide some guarantees as to his punctuality, discipline, judicious behaviour. Employers, especially in advertising, not only decline to take on people over the age of thirty-five, they are reluctant to rely on someone who, at the age of thirty, has never been *on the staff*. No question, either, of carrying on using them as if nothing had changed, on short-term contracts: such instability looks unconvincing; at thirty, you owe it to yourself to have got somewhere, or else you are nowhere. And no-one is anywhere unless he has found his niche, built his nest, got his own keys, his own desk, his own little name-plate.

Jérôme and Sylvie thought often about this problem. They still had a few years left, but the life they led, the entirely relative peace they enjoyed, would never be a permanent possession. Everything would crumble progressively; they would have nothing left. They did not feel crushed by their work, they were sure of a living, more or less, for better or worse, taking the rough with the smooth, without their profession consuming the whole of their lives. But that was not destined to last.

You can never remain just a market researcher for very long. Almost as soon as they are trained, researchers rush towards the higher rungs, to become deputy director or director of an agency, or to find one of those coveted jobs in some big firm, as director of, say, recruitment, or staff training, or industrial relations. These are the plum jobs: carpeted offices, two telephones, a dictaphone, a refrigerated cocktail cabinet and even, sometimes, hanging on the wall, a painting by Bernard Buffet.

Alas, said Jérôme and Sylvie to themselves very often and sometimes to each other, you have to work to earn your crust, that's obvious, but if you work you do not live. They thought they had learned that, in years gone by, from experience, of a few weeks' duration. Sylvie had become a filing clerk in a market research consultancy, whilst Jérôme coded and decoded interview questionnaires. Their working conditions were more than pleasant. They turned up when they liked, read the newspapers in the office, went down for a beer or a coffee quite often, and they even felt a degree of liking for the work they performed in dilatory fashion, led on as they were by an exceedingly vague promise of proper employment on a regular contract and accelerated promotion. But they didn't stick it out for very long. They were atrociously grumpy on getting up; full of resentment every evening, going home on the overcrowded metro; they would slump onto their sofa, dog-tired and dirty, and do nothing but dream of long weekends, free days and not getting up in the morning.

They felt locked in, trapped, done for. They could not resign themselves to such a fate. They still believed that masses of things could happen to them, that it was the fixed daily hours of work, the unending sequence of days and weeks that made the straitjacket which they did not hesitate to describe as infernal. It was, all the same, and whatever else might be said about it, the start of a fine career: it held out good prospects for them; they were at that epic stage when the boss assesses you as a youngster, feels privately pleased with himself for having taken you on, gets straight down to training you, to shaping you in his own image, invites you to dinner, gives you a friendly thump, and, with a wave of his hand, opens your door to fortune.

They were stupid – how many times did they repeat to themselves that they were stupid, that they were wrong, that they were in any case no more right than the others, the ones who hang on determinedly and climb? – but they liked their long days of idleness, their lazy wakings, their mornings in bed, with a pile of detective novels and science-fiction beside them, they liked their walks in the night, down by the riverside, and the almost elating sense of freedom that they felt on some days, the feeling of holiday time which overcame them each time they got back from a campaign in the provinces.

Of course they knew that was all wrong, that their freedom was just a will o' the wisp. Their lives were much more marked by almost panic-stricken hunting for work each time (and there were many) one of the agencies they worked for went bust or got taken over by a bigger firm, by their days before pay when cigarettes had to be counted out one by one, by the time it took, on some days, to get invited out for a meal.

They were right in the middle of the most idiotic, the most ordinary predicament in the world. But knowing it was idiotic and ordinary did not prevent them being right in it. Long ago, they had let slip, work and freedom had ceased to be strict opposites; all the same, it was that opposition which was, for them, the determining factor.

People who choose to earn money first, people who put off their *real* plans until later, until they are rich, are not necessarily wrong. People who want only to live, and who reckon living is absolute freedom, the exclusive pursuit of happiness, the sole satisfaction of their desires and instincts, the immediate enjoyment of the boundless riches of the world – Jérôme and Sylvie had taken on this vast pro-gramme for themselves – such people will always be un-happy. It is true, they would admit, that there are people for whom this kind of dilemma does not arise, or hardly arises, either because they are too poor and have no require-ments beyond a slightly better diet, slightly better housing, slightly less work, or because they are too rich, from the start, to understand the import or even the meaning of such a distinction. But nowadays and in our part of the world, more and more people are neither rich nor poor: they dream of wealth, and could become wealthy; and that is where their misfortunes begin.

Let us take a young man who does a year or two at university, then completes his military service honourably.

Around the age of twenty-five, there he is, as naked as the day he was born, although he is also, by virtue of his education, already in virtual possession of more money than he ever wished for. That is to say, he knows with certainty that the day will come when he will have his flat in the city, his country cottage, his car, his hi-fi. It so happens, however, that these elating promises continue to evade his actual grasp. By their very nature they belong to a process which also includes, if you care to think about it, marriage, parenthood, a change in values, social attitudes and patterns of personal behaviour. In short, our young man will have to settle down, and it will take him fifteen years.

Such a prospect is not comforting. No-one embarks upon it without protest. For Christ's sake, our young lad thinks, am I going to have to spend my days behind these glass walls instead of going for walks in flowery meadows? am I going to catch myself hoping the night before each promotion exercise? am I going to calculate, connive, champ my bit, me, who used to dream of poetry, of night trains, of warm sandy beaches? And, taking it mistakenly to be a consolation, he falls into the trap of hire-purchase. Then he is caught, well and truly caught. All he can do is to gird up his patience. Alas, when he gets to the end of his troubles, our young man is no longer quite so young, and, to cap his misfortune, it can even seem to him that his life is behind him, that it consisted only of his striving and not of what he strove for, and even if he is too cautious, too sensible – his slow climb has given him plenty of experience – to dare to say such things to himself, it will none the less be true that he will be forty, and straightening out his home and his weekend place and his children's education will have filled more than adequately the few hours he will have been able to spare from his work . . .

★

Impatience, thought Jérôme and Sylvie, is a twentieth-century virtue. At twenty, when they saw, or thought they saw, what life could be, the sum of bliss it held, the endless conquests it allowed, etc., they realised they would not have the strength to wait. Like anyone else, they could have made it; but all they wanted was to have it made. That is probably the sense in which they were what are commonly called intellectuals.

For everything contradicted them, beginning with life itself. They wanted life's enjoyment, but all around them enjoyment was equated with ownership. They wanted to stay free, and virtually innocent, but time went by notwithstanding, and brought them nothing. The others ended up seeing wealth as an end in itself, but as for them, they didn't have any money at all.

They told themselves they weren't the worst off. Perhaps they were right. But modern life irritated their misfortune whilst it erased the misfortunes of others: the others were on the right track. Jérôme and Sylvie didn't amount to much: penny-scrabblers, freelancers, flitters. On the other hand, time, in a certain sense, was actually on their side, they had an image of a possible world which could seem exhilarating. But this, they agreed, was, by way of consolation, pretty small beer.

VI

They had put down roots in a temporary soil. They did their work in the way others study, choosing their own hours. They could waste time like only students can.

But on all sides dangers lurked. They would have liked their story to be a story of happiness; but more often than not it was a tale of happiness under threat. They were still young, but the years were going by fast. An old student is a gruesome thing; a burnt-out case is more gruesome still. They were afraid.

They had free time; but time was also working against them. There were bills for gas, electricity and the telephone that had to be paid. Every day they had to eat. They had to have clothes, they had to redecorate, change the sheets, take the washing to the laundry, gets shirts ironed, buy shoes, catch the train, buy furniture.

Money, sometimes, consumed them entirely. They did not stop thinking about it. Even their emotional life, to a considerable extent, depended on it directly. There was every reason to think that when they had a little wealth, when they got a breathing space, their shared happiness was indestructible, no constraint appeared to limit their love. Their tastes, imagination, new ideas and appetites blended indistinguishably into freedom. But these were privileged moments; more often they had to struggle: at the first signs of overspending, quite often they would rise up against each other. They would clash over nothing, for a wasted one hundred old francs, for a pair of stockings, for not doing the washing-up. Then for hours on end, for whole days at a stretch, they stopped speaking to each other. They would dine hurriedly, opposite one another, each for himself, for herself, not looking. They would sit at opposite ends of the sofa, half-turning their backs on each other. One or the other would play patience, interminably.

Money stood like a barrier between them. It was a wall, a kind of buffer they banged against at every turn. It was something worse than poverty: a narrow, straitened, exiguous absence of ease. They inhabited the closed world of their closed lives, without a future, without openings other than impossible miracles, stupid dreams which wouldn't hold water. They were suffocating. They felt they were sinking.

They could of course talk of other things, about a recent book, a theatre director, about the war in Algeria or about people, but it sometimes felt as if their only *real* conversations were about money, comfort and happiness. That was when their voices would rise, the tension grow. They would talk and, as they talked, they would feel just how impossible, unreachable and paltry these things were. They would grow irritated; they were over-anxious; they would feel implicitly challenged, each by the other. They would dream up holiday plans, travel plans, plans for the flat, and then tear them down, rabidly: it would seem as if what was most real in their lives would then appear in its true light as something without substance, something absent. So they would fall silent, and their silence was full of rancour; they resented life and sometimes were weak enough to resent each other; they remembered their messed-up degrees, their unappealing holidays, their drab life, their cluttered flat, their impossible dreams. They

67

would look at each other, they would find the other partner ugly, badly dressed, graceless, crumpled. Beside them, in the street, cars slid slowly on. In the city squares, the neon lights flashed in turn. At the café terraces, people looked like complacent fish. They hated the world. They went home on foot, tired out. They went to bed without saying a word.

If some day something were to give way, such as an agency going out of business or their being seen as too old, or too unreliable in their work, or one of them falling ill, that was all it would take for everything to come tumbling down. They had no prospects, no reserves. Their minds often turned to this subject, anxiously. They would come back to it incessantly, in spite of themselves. They could see themselves out of work for months on end, taking on penny jobs just to survive, borrowing, begging. Then, sometimes, they would experience moments of intense despair. They would dream of offices, of established posts, of regular hours, of proper contracts of employment. But these reversed images threw them into perhaps even greater despair. They just could not, so they thought, recognise themselves in the face of a desk-bound executive, however splendid his apparel. They decided that they detested hierarchies, and that solutions, miraculous or other, would come from elsewhere, from the world, from History. They went on in their bumpy way; it fitted their natural inclination. In an imperfect world, of this they convinced themselves easily, it was not by any means the most imperfect way. They lived for the day; in six hours they would spend what it had taken three days to earn; they often borrowed; they ate ghastly French fries, smoked their last cigarette between them, sometimes spent two hours looking for a spare metro ticket, wore recycled shirts, listened to scratched records, hitch-hiked to get places, and, quite frequently still, put off changing the sheets for five or six weeks. They were quite near to believing that, all in all, this kind of life was not without its charm.

VII

When they talked to each other about their kind of living, their way of life, their future – when they surrendered themselves in a kind of frenzy, and entirely, to an orgy of better worlds – they sometimes said, with a rather hollow melancholy, that they had not sorted things out properly in their minds. They saw the world through muddled eyes, and the clarity they proclaimed as a value was often accompanied by indecisive fluctuations, ambiguous compromises and assorted other considerations which modulated, minimised or even undermined entirely what were, quite obviously still, their good intentions.

It seemed to them that there they had found a path, or an absence of path, which defined them perfectly, and not just them but all those of their age. Earlier generations, they would sometimes tell each other, had probably found it possible to reach a fuller awareness of themselves and of the world they lived in. They would have liked, perhaps, to have been twenty during the Spanish Civil War, or during the Resistance: in fact, they talked about it a great deal; it seemed to them that the problems facing people then, the problems they imagined people facing, were clearer, even if the need to respond had turned out to be more pressing. As for themselves, the questions that faced them were all booby-traps.

Their nostalgia was slightly hypocritical. The Algerian war had begun with them and was being pursued before their eyes. It hardly affected them; they took action on occasions, but they rarely felt obliged to do so. For years they didn't imagine that their lives, their future, their ideas might one day be turned upside down by it. But that is what happened, up to a point, at one time in the past: in their student days they had come to participate more spontaneously and often almost enthusiastically in the meetings and street demonstrations which had greeted the outbreak of the war, the call-up of the reserve, and, especially, the coming of Gaullism. In those days there seemed to be a connection, directly established, between what they did in their own small sphere and what they aimed to do. And you couldn't really reproach them for having been, as it turned out, quite wrong: the war didn't cease, Gaullism didn't go away. Jérôme and Sylvie dropped their studies. In advertising circles – which were generally located by quasi-mythical tradition to the left of centre, but were rather better defined by technocracy, the cult of efficiency, modernity, complexity, by the taste for speculating on future trends and by the more demagogic strain in sociology, as well as by the still very widespread opinion that nine-tenths of the population were fools just able to sing the praises of anything or anybody in unison – in advertising circles, then, it was fashionable to despise all merely topical political issues and to grasp History in nothing smaller than centuries. It happened to be the case, furthermore, that Gaullism was an adequate response, an infinitely more dynamic response than people had at first declared far and wide that it would be, and that its danger lay always in some other place than the one where people thought they had found it.

The war dragged on all the same, even if they saw it only as an episode, as a fact of an almost secondary nature. They had a bad conscience about it, of course. But their feeling of responsibility went no deeper than their memory of having been affected by it in the past, than a virtually

71

automatic allegiance to moral imperatives of a very broad and unspecific kind. Such indifference could have given them a measure of the true strength of many of their bursts of passion – of their pointlessness, even perhaps of their gutlessness. But the real question lay elsewhere. They had watched with something approaching surprise as some of their old friends got themselves involved, cautiously or wholeheartedly, in helping the FLN, the Algerian freedom fighters. They hadn't really grasped why, and could not manage to take seriously either the romantic explanation (which tended, rather, to make them smile) or the political explanation, which passed their understanding almost entirely. As for themselves, they had solved the problem far more simply: Jérôme and three of his friends, relying on valuable contacts in high places and fraudulent doctors' certificates, had managed to get themselves exempted from military service in time, on health grounds.

Yet it was the war in Algeria and the war alone which for almost two years protected them from themselves. After all, they might have aged less well, or less slowly. But it was not by their own decisions, nor by acts of their own volition, nor even, whatever they might have claimed, by their sense of humour that they succeeded for some considerable time in deferring a future which they painted, self-indulgently, in blackest hue. The events of 1961 and 1962 – from the Algiers generals' putsch to the massacre at Charonne metro station – which heralded the end of the war enabled them, temporarily but with uncommon effectiveness, to forget, or rather, to suspend their habitual concerns. Their gloomiest forecasts, their fear of never making it, of ending up in some obscure and narrow rut, looked a good deal less dreadful, on some days, than what was happening before their eyes, than what threatened them day by day.

Those were sad and violent times. Housewives stocked up with sugar in kilos, bottles of cooking oil, tins of tuna, coffee and condensed milk. Squads of helmeted security policemen in shiny black waterproof capes and service boots patrolled at ease up and down Boulevard Sebastopol, carrying cavalry rifles.

Because the back seats of their cars were often strewn with a few out-of-date issues of newspapers which some touchy individuals could be expected to consider demoralising, subversive or just plain liberal – *Le Monde*, *Libération*, *France-Observateur* – Jérôme and Sylvie and their friends fell prey on occasions to furtive fears and worrying hallucinations: they were being followed, their number-plates were being taken down, they were being watched, being framed: five wine-sodden foreign legionnaires were going to set upon them and leave them for dead in a dark alley, on the rain-washed pavement, in a neighbourhood of ill repute . . .

Thus martyrdom burst into their daily lives, became, on occasions, an obsession and, it seemed to them, a characteristic of a particular group attitude, and it gave the days, the events and the thoughts of this time their specific colouring. Visions of blood, of explosions, violence and terror went with them always. It might seem on some days that they were ready for anything; but the next day life would be precarious, the future bleak. They would dream of exile, of the countryside, of long cruises. They wished they could live in England, where policemen are reputed to behave with respect for the individual. And all through that winter, as the cease-fire drew nearer and nearer, they would dream of the coming spring, of holidays to come, of the year ahead when, as the papers said, fratricidal passions would have subsided, when it would be possible once again to saunter, to go out at night on foot with your mind at rest and your body safe and sound.

The pressure of events led them to take a stand. They were committed, of course, only superficially. Their political consciousness, insofar as they had any such thing as a structured and considered set of thoughts rather than an inchoate eruption of more or less consistently angled opinions, was, they thought, already beyond or above the Algerian issue, engaged with alternatives that were more utopian than real, with general questions which, they conceded with some regret, had little chance of producing any kind of practical result. None the less, they joined the Anti-Fascist Committee which had just been set up in their area. They rose, on occasions, at five in the morning, to go out, with three or four comrades, pasting up posters calling on people to be alert, denouncing the guilty and their stooges, protesting at outrages and honouring the innocent victims. They took petitions round all the houses in their street, and, three or four times, did guard duty in threatened premises.

They took part in some demonstrations. On such days, there were buses on the streets without number-plates, cafés would shut early, people would hurry home. They were frightened all day long. They went out feeling uneasy. It was five o'clock and a thin drizzle was falling. They looked at the other demonstrators, smiling tensely, sought out their friends, tried to talk about other things. The marchers formed into columns, which moved forward, then came to a standstill. From the midst of the crowd they were in, they could see, in front of them, a great expanse of wet and gloomy tarmac and then, taking up the whole width of the boulevard, the thick black line of the Riot Police. Cohorts of midnight-blue pantechnicons with wire netting over their windows processed in the distance. They dragged their feet, holding hands, dripping with sweat, scarcely daring to shout, and ran off as soon as the first signal was given.

It didn't add up to much. They were the first to be aware of this, and they often wondered, standing in the middle of the pack, what they were doing there, out in the cold, in the rain, in these sinister parts of the town – Bastille, Nation, Hôtel de Ville. They wished something would happen to prove that what they were doing was important, necessary, irreplaceable, that their fear-struck efforts would have a meaning for them, would be something they needed, something that might help them to know themselves, to change themselves, to live. No: their real lives were elsewhere, in a near or distant future also full of menace, but of a more subtle, less straightforward kind: traps you could not touch, spellbound webs.

The attempted assassination at Issy-les-Moulineaux and the brief demonstration which followed it marked the end of their militant activities. Their local Anti-Fascist Committee held one more meeting and agreed to step up its activity. But, as the holiday season was nearly upon them, there didn't really seem to be any good reason for them even to remain vigilant.

VIII

They could not have said exactly what it was that changed when the war ended. For a long time it was as if the only impression they could feel was the sense of an ending, of something completed or concluded. Not a happy ending, not a dramatic resolution, but quite the opposite, a melancholy, dying fall, which left behind it feelings of emptiness, of bitterness, memories clouded over by darkness. Time had passed, time had fled; an era was over; peace had returned, a peace they had never known; the war came to an end. At a stroke, seven years tipped into history: their student years, their years of making friends, the best years of their lives.

Maybe nothing had changed. They would still sometimes stand at their window, looking at the courtyard, the tiny gardens, the chestnut tree, listening to the birds singing. Other books, other records were now piled up on their rickety bookshelves. The gramophone needle was beginning to wear out.

Their work had stayed the same. They were doing the same surveys as three years before. What do you shave with? Do you put polish on your shoes? They had seen films, and seen films again, they had travelled, and discovered other restaurants. They had bought shirts and shoes, jumpers and skirts, plates, sheets and trinkets.

What was new was terribly insidious, terribly vague, terribly bound up with their own unique story, with their dreams. They were weary. They had aged; yes, they had.

Some days they felt as if they still hadn't begun to live. But the life they were leading came more and more to seem to them a precarious and ephemeral thing; and they felt drained of strength, as if their waiting, their hardships, their pinched budgets had worn them out, as if all of it – unsatisfied desires, imperfect pleasures, wasted time – had been in the natural order of things.

On occasions they wished everything would stay the same, not ever move. Then they would be able just to drift. Their life would keep them warm: it would stretch ahead through the months and years without – or almost without – altering, without ever hampering them. It would be but the harmonious sequence of their days and nights, the one almost imperceptibly modulating the other, a never-ending reprise of the same themes, a continuous happiness, a perpetuated enjoyment which no upset, no tragic event, no twist or turn of fate would ever bring into question.

At other times they could not stand it a moment longer. They wanted to fight, and to win. But how could they fight? Whom would they fight? What should they fight? They lived in a strange and shimmering world, the bedazzling universe of a market culture, in prisons of plenty, in the bewitching traps of comfort and happiness.

Where were the dangers? Where were the threats? In the past men fought in their millions, and millions still do fight, for their crust of bread. Jérôme and Sylvie did not quite believe you could go into battle for a chesterfield settee. But that was all the same the banner under which they would have enlisted most readily. There was nothing, they thought, that concerned them in party manifestos or in government plans: they would sneer at early retirement pension schemes, increased holiday entitlements, free lunches, the thirty-hour week. They wanted superabundance – Garrard turntables, empty beaches for their eyes only, round-the-world trips, grand hotels.

The enemy was unseen. Or, rather, the enemy was within them, it had rotted them, infected them, eaten them away. They were the hollow men, the turkey round the stuffing. Tame pets, faithfully reflecting a world which taunted them. They were up to their necks in a cream cake from which they would only ever be able to nibble crumbs.

For years the crises they had encountered had scarcely dented their good humour. They hadn't taken them as inevitable or terminal affairs; they were crises in which nothing was at stake. They often reflected that friendship was protecting them. The group held together, reliably, cohesively, it was a firm guarantee of their stability, a force they could count on. They were sure they were right because they knew they would stick together, and they liked nothing more than to be together at one or another's flat towards the end of an especially awkward month, sitting around a tureen of potatoes and bacon, sharing their last cigarettes as fraternally as it was possible to do.

But friendships, too, began to fray. Some evenings, within the finite fields of their unspacious rooms, the couples that had come together crossed swords by word and eye. Some evenings, they finally grasped that their fine friendships, their almost hermetic language, their private jokes, this shared world, shared language, the common gestures they had made up, were based on nothing: theirs was a shrunken universe, a world running out of steam, opening onto nothing. Their lives were not conquests, but slow collapses, dispersions. That was when they realised how deeply they were condemned to habit, to sluggishness. They were bored in each other's company as if all there had ever been between them was a void. Puns, boozing, walks in the woods, dinner parties, endless discussions about films, plans, gossip had long stood in for adventure, history and truth. But the words were hollow, the gestures empty, without substance, without consequence, without a future, words repeated a thousand times, hands shaken a thousand times, ritual actions which no longer afforded them any protection.

At that time they would spend an hour trying to agree about which film they would go to see. They would talk just for the sake of talking, play at riddles or at guessing games. Each couple, when alone, would speak harshly of the others and sometimes of themselves; they would harp on their lost youth; they would recall having once been enthusiastic, spontaneous, brim-full of real plans, of images of wealth, of desires. They would dream of new friendships; but they could barely manage to picture them.

Slowly but with inexorable obviousness, the group fell apart. With sometimes brutal suddenness, in the space of barely a few weeks, it became obvious to some of them that the life of old would never again be on. Their weariness was too great. The outside world too demanding. People who had lived in rooms with no running water, who had dined on a quarter of a stick-loaf, who had believed they were living as they pleased, who had burnt the candle at both ends without running out of wick, such people, one fine day, settled down. They were swayed, almost naturally, almost objectively, by the temptation of a steady job, a staff appointment, bonus payments, and an extra salary cheque at Christmas.

One after another almost all their friends gave in. The age of rootless living gave way to the age of security. We simply cannot, they would say, go on like this all our lives. And they said *like this* with a vague wave of the hand towards: larking about, too little sleep, eating potatoes, worn-out jackets, hard work on low pay, public transport.

Bit by bit and without really noticing it happen, Jérôme and Sylvie ended up almost alone. Friendship was possible, it seemed to them, only when they were in the same boat, leading the same lives. But when one couple suddenly acquires what looks to the other couple like a fortune, or the firm prospect of a fortune, whilst the other, for its part, prizes the freedom it has clung to – there was what felt like a clash of two worlds. It was no longer a matter of passing squabbles, but of real splits, deep chasms, of wounds that would not close up all by themselves. Mistrust of a sort that would have been impossible a few months earlier had entered their relationships. They would be stand-offish in conversation; they seemed to be for ever challenging each other.

Jérôme and Sylvie were harsh, were unfair about their friends. They spoke of treason and abdication. They took pleasure in observing at first hand the devastating damage which money, they claimed, would wreak upon those who had sacrificed everything on its altar, and from which damage they were, they thought, still exempt. They watched their old friends settle almost easily, almost too comfortably, into rigid hierarchies and unreservedly adopt the values of the world they were entering. They watched them scrape and wheedle and come to believe in their power, their influence, their responsibilities. Through them they believed they could see the exact opposite of their own world: the one which gave justification, all together, to money, work, advertising, skills, a world which gave value to experience, a world which gave them no place, the solemn world of executives, the world of power. They came close to believing that their friends were being taken for a ride.

They did not despise money. Perhaps it was the opposite: that they loved it too much. They would have liked substance, certainty, a calm, clear way to the future. They were alert to all signs of permanence: they wanted to be rich. And if they still refused to make themselves rich, it was because they did not need a salary. Their imagination, their culture allowed them to think only in millions.

They often went out in the evening, sniffing the air, ogling the window displays. They would push on past the thirteenth *arrondissement*, close to home, and of which they knew only Avenue des Gobelins because of its four cinemas, they would skirt around the sinister Rue Cuvier which would have led them only to the even more sinister environs of Gare d'Austerlitz, and, almost naturally, would follow Rue Monge, then Rue des Ecoles, on to Saint-Michel, Saint-Germain, and thence, according to their whim or the time of year, to Palais-Royal, Opéra, Montparnasse, Vavin, Rue d'Assas, Saint-Sulpice, the Luxembourg gardens. They walked slowly. They stopped at each antique dealer's, pressed their noses against ill-lit windows, made out, through the mesh shutters, the reddish glow of a leather sofa, the foliate decoration of an earthenware dish or plate, the gleam of cut glass or a brass candlestick, the elegant curve of a cane-seated chair.

From one station to another – antique dealer, bookshops, record shops, restaurant menus, travel agencies, shirt-makers, tailors, cheese-shops, bootmakers, confectioners, delicatessens, stationers – their paths through Paris constituted their real universe: in them lay their ambitions and hopes. That was where real life was, the life they wanted to know, that they wanted to lead: was it not for these salmon, for these carpets, for these crystal glasses that, twenty-five years before, a shopgirl and a ladies' hairdresser had brought the two of them into this world?

The next morning, when life once more ground away at them, when the great advertising machine in which they were tiny cogs once more started up, they would not have forgotten entirely, it seemed to them, the blurred treasures, the unveiled secrets of their fervent night-time quest. They would sit opposite people who believed in the brands, the jingles, the images that were put in front of them, people who ate the dripping from beef bought in from a knacker's yard and found its hazelnut fragrance and plant-like odour quite delicious. (But did they themselves – without knowing really why, and with an odd, almost worrisome feeling that they were not quite grasping something – did they not admire some posters, find some slogans marvellous, reckon some trailers were brilliant?) They would sit down and switch on their tape-recorders, they would say ah and hm with the right intonation, they would fake their interviews, bungle their reports, they would be dreaming, muddle-headedly, of something else.

IX

How could they make their fortune? They could find no solution to the problem. And yet, every day, so it seemed, there were individuals who managed to solve it for themselves. And these examples to be followed, these wise and smiling, sly and wilful faces full of health, firmness and modesty upholding to eternity the moral and intellectual resilience of the French nation, were nothing less than icons instilling patience and right feelings in the others, in the ones who lagged behind, who stood still, champed their bit, bit the dust.

They knew all there was to know about the rise of such men kissed by Fortune – captains of industry, incorruptible, glittering prize-winners from Ecole Polytechnique, financial wizards, men of letters without a smudge, globe-trotting pioneers, packet-soup salesmen, suburban developers, crooners, playboys, gold-diggers, jugglers of Mammon. They had simple stories. They were still young and had kept their good looks, with that dull gleam of experience in their eyes, greying hair on their temples to show for their years of struggle, with frank, engaging smiles concealing sharp teeth, double-jointed fingers, seductive voices.

They could easily imagine themselves fitting into such a role. They would have a three-acter in a bottom drawer. Their garden plot would be sitting on oil, or uranium. They would live for years in poverty, hardship, doubt. They would dream of going first-class, just once, on the

metro. And then, suddenly, brutally, wildly, unexpect-
edly, like a thunderclap: fortune! Their play would be
accepted, their mineral deposit discovered, their genius
acclaimed. Contracts would rain down, and they would
light their havanas with thousand-franc banknotes.

It would be a morning like any other. Under the front
door three envelopes would have been slipped: long and
narrow, with impressive embossed official lettering and
the address accurately typed in with perfect spacing on an
IBM Executive. Their hands would shake a little as they
opened them. There would be three cheques with long
strings of numbers on them. Or else a letter:

> "Dear Sir
> Your uncle, Mr Palmgrease, having died
> intestate . . ."

and they would pass their hands over their faces, not
believing their eyes and thinking they were still dreaming;
they would open the window wide.

Thus did they dream, stupidly, happily, of inheritances,
jackpots, winning at the races. Someone would break the
bank at Monte Carlo; they would find a satchel abandoned
in the luggage rack of some empty railway carriage, stuffed
with wads of high-denomination notes; in a dozen oysters,
enough pearls to make a string. Or a couple of Boulle
armchairs bought off an illiterate peasant in Poitou.

They would be carried away by great surges. Sometimes,
for hours on end, for days at a stretch, a frenzy of desire
to be rich, immediately, enormously and for ever, would
seize them and hold them in its grip. It was an insane,
unwholesome, oppressive desire which seemed to control
their slightest movement. Fortune became their opium. It

intoxicated them. They surrendered unreservedly to the delirium of their fantasies. Wherever they went they paid heed only to money. They had nightmares of millions of gems.

They would attend the big auctions at Drouot and Galliera. They would mingle with gentlemen examining pictures, catalogue in hand. They watched Degas pastels, rare postage stamps, stupid gold coins, fragile editions of La Fontaine and Crébillon luxuriously bound by Lederer, admirable pieces of furniture bearing the mark of Claude Séné or Oehlenberg, gold or enamel snuff-boxes, being sold off. The auctioneer presented the lots in turn; some people with serious faces went to cast an eye over them; murmurs passed through the crowd. The bidding began. Prices climbed. Then the hammer fell, and it was over, the object disappeared, five or ten million francs had gone by within reach of their hands.

Sometimes they trailed the new owners; these happy mortals were most often only underlings, antique-dealers' buyers, private secretaries, straw men. They would be led by them to the portals of austere mansions in Voie Oswaldo-Cruz, Boulevard Beauséjour, Rue Maspéro, Rue Spontini, Villa Saïd, Avenue du Roule. Beyond the railings, box shrubberies, and gravelled drives, incompletely drawn curtains sometimes gave them a glimpse of large, barely-lit rooms. They could make out vaguely the shapes of the sofas and armchairs, the blurred brushstrokes of an impressionist painting. And they would beat their retreat, wistful and grumpy.

One day they even dreamed of stealing. They imagined, at length, dressing in black and, with a tiny flashlight in one hand and a jemmy and a glass-cutter in their pocket, entering a building after nightfall, getting into the cellars, forcing the primitive lock on a dumb-waiter, reaching the kitchens. It would be a flat belonging to a diplomat on service overseas, of a shady financier with nonetheless perfect taste, of a distinguished dilettante, of an enlightened art-lover. They would know every nook and cranny. They would know where to find the little twelfth-century Madonna, the oval panel by Sebastiano del Piombo, the Fragonard wash drawing, the two small Renoirs, the little Boudin, the Atlan, the Max Ernst, the de Staels, the coins, the musical boxes, the candyboxes, the silverware, the Delft china. They would move with precision and firmness, as if they had rehearsed it all many times over. They would move unhurriedly, confidently, efficiently, imperturbably, phlegmatically: the Arsène Lupins of modern times. Not a muscle of their faces would twitch. One by one the showcases would be broken into; one by one the canvases would be taken down and removed from their frames.

Their car would be waiting below. They would have filled the tank the day before. Their passports would be in order. They would have had preparations for departure in hand for a long while. Their trunks would be in Brussels already. They would take the Flanders road, cross the Belgian border without hindrance. Then, little by little, without undue haste, in Luxemburg, in Antwerp, Amsterdam, London, the States, South America, they would sell off their booty. They would go round the world. They would wander for years, as the whim took them. They would settle eventually in a land with a pleasant climate. They would buy, somewhere, in the Italian lakes, or at Dubrovnik, in the Balearics, or Cefalù, a large, white stone house nestling in the middle of a park.

They didn't do anything of the sort, of course. They didn't even buy a lottery ticket. At the very most they put into their poker games – a game they discovered at that time and which was set to become the last port of call for their creaky friendships – a relentlessness which at times could look suspicious. Some weeks they played as many as three or four games, each one of which kept them up until the small hours. They played for small stakes, so small that they had only the foretaste of risk and the semblance of winnings. And yet, when, with two low pairs or, even better, with a four-card flush, they threw on the table, at one go, a hatful of chips worth at least three hundred (old) francs and scooped the pool, when they had upped the ante to six hundred francs' worth of IOU's, lost them in three calls, then won them – and more – back again in six calls, a modest smile of triumph would light their faces. They had pushed lady luck their way; their sliver of courage had borne fruit; they were not far short of feeling like heroes.

X

A farming survey took them all over France. They went to Lorraine, Saintonge, Picardy, Beauce, Limagne. They met lawyers of ancient stock, wholesalers whose lorries covered a quarter of France, prosperous industrialists, gentlemen-farmers always escorted by a pack of big russet dogs and watchful factors.

The silos were full of wheat. In great cobbled courtyards sparkling tractors faced the squires' black saloon cars. They passed through the workers' canteen, the vast kitchen where women toiled, the great hall with its yellowing floor – where no-one went without first replacing his shoes with felt slippers – and its massive fireplace, its television set, its wing-chairs, light oak chests, brasses, pewter, china plate. Along a narrow passage impregnated with smells they came to a door opening on to an office. It almost seemed a small room, so great was the clutter. Beside an old hand-operated telephone mounted on the wall, a year planner summed up the life of a farming business: cereals to be planted, plans, estimates, account days; a graph gave eloquent testimony to record yields. On a table piled high with receipts, payslips, memos and bumph, a black, cloth-bound ledger, open at that day's page, gave sight of long columns of figures, of flourishing finances. Framed certificates – for bulls, milking cows, prize sows – jostled with bits of land-registry charts, ordnance survey maps, portrait photographs of herds and farmyards and four-colour-printed prospectuses for tractors, threshers, grubbers and drills.

That was where they plugged in their tape-recorders. They made grave enquiries about the changing place of agriculture in the modern world, the contradictions of the French countryside, the farmer of tomorrow, the Common Market, government rulings on wheat and beet, free-range methods and floor prices. But their minds were somewhere else. They could see themselves coming and going in the house when it had been abandoned. They would go up polished stairs, enter shuttered and musty bedrooms. Beneath dun canvas dustcovers would be venerable pieces of furniture. They would open nine-foot-high wardrobes full of lavender-scented linen, preserving jars and silverware.

In the half-light of attics they would discover unsuspected treasure. In unending cellars they would be welcomed by tuns and hogsheads, vats full of oil and honey, barrels of preserves in brine, juniper-roast ham, kegs of rough brandy.

They would saunter through echoing laundry rooms, through wood stores, through coal stores, through fruit storerooms where endless rows of apples and pears would be laid out on wicker trays stacked on top of each other, through dairies with their unmistakable smell, where mountains of freshly-made pats of butter would display their glorious, still dripping, maker's mark, alongside churns of milk, pancheons of fresh cream, cottage cheese, quark.

They would go on through cowsheds, stables, workshops, forges, barns, ovens where huge lumps of dough were baking, warehouses bursting with sacks, tractor sheds.

From the top of the water-tower, they would be able to see the whole farmhouse enclosing on all four sides the great cobbled courtyard with its two pointed-arch gateways, its backyard, piggery, kitchen garden, orchard, the avenue of plane trees marking the track that leads to the main road, and, all around, as far as the eye could see, the great striped yellowness of wheatfields, the thickets, the pasture land, the straight black lines of the roads on which, occasionally, you could see the passing glint of a car, and the wavy line of poplars all along a deeply embanked, almost invisible river, stretching to misty hills on the far horizon.

Then, in gusts, other mirages swirled. They saw vast open markets, endlessly long arcades of shops, unbelievable restaurants. Everything man can eat, everything that could be drunk, was laid out before them. Chests, crates, baskets, trays spilling over with fat, yellow or red apples, squat pears, purple grapes. Stalls of mangoes, figs, honeydew and water melon, lemons, pomegranates, sacks of almonds, walnuts, pistachios, punnets of raisins and sultanas, dried bananas, candied fruits, yellow and transparent dried dates.

There were *charcuteries*, colonnaded temples with ceilings groaning with hams and sausages, dark caverns piled high with *pâtés* and black puddings coiled up like ships' hawsers, barrels of sauerkraut, of purplish olives, of salted anchovies, of sweet-pickled cucumber.

Or else, on both sides of an alley, double ranks of suckling pigs and wild boars hanging by their feet, half-sides of beef, hares, fatted geese, deer with glazed eyes.

They would pass through delicatessens redolent with delicious smells, wondrous *pâtisseries* with hundreds of tarts in a row, magnificent kitchens with a thousand copper cauldrons.

They would drown in plenty. They dreamed up huge market halls. Before their eyes arose Eldorados of hams, cheeses and spirits. Tables set themselves fully laden, bedecked with sparkling white tablecloths, strewn with flowers, covered with cut glass and fine plate. There were *pâtés en croûte* by the dozen, *terrines*, salmon, pike, trout, lobster, dressed legs of lamb with horn- and silver-handled decorations, hare and quail, steaming boar, cheeses the size of millstones, regiments of bottles.

Locomotives would appear hauling freight cars loaded with fatted cattle; lorries bearing bleating ewes would draw up, baskets of crayfish would be piled up in pyramids. Millions of loaves would emerge from a thousand ovens. Tons of coffee beans would be unloaded from ships' holds.

Then, even further on – their eyes would be half closed now – amidst forests and lawns, by river banks, at the gates of the desert or on a cliff overlooking the sea, on great squares paved with marble, they would see skyscrapers rise one hundred storeys high.

They would wander by their walls of steel, tropical wood, glass and marble. In the central foyer, all along a cut-glass partition beaming millions of rainbows throughout the building, a waterfall would spout from the fifth-floor level, encircled by the dizzy spiral of twin aluminium stairwells.

Lifts bore them upwards. They went down curving corridors, walked up crystal steps, through luminous galleries where statues and flowers stood in lines as far as the eye could see, where limpid brooks flowed on beds of polychrome pebbles.

Doors opened in front of them. They came upon open-air swimming pools, patios, reading rooms, quiet rooms, theatres, aviaries, gardens, aquariums, tiny museums for their sole use where, on the four canted sides of a small room with cut-off corners, four Flemish portraits were hung. Some rooms were all rock, others all jungle; in others, the sea broke in waves; and in others, peacocks paraded. From the ceiling of a circular room hung thousands of oriflammes. Inexhaustible mazes echoed with sweet music; one room with an outlandish shape served no other purpose, it seemed, than to set off unending echoes. The floor of another room represented at different times of the day the different stages in a very complicated game.

In the enormous basement, as far as the eye could see, docile machinery worked away.

They would drift from marvel to marvel, from surprise to surprise. All they had to do was to live, to be there, for the world to offer itself to them whole. Their ships, their trains, their rockets crisscrossed the planet. The world was in their arms, with its wheat-covered counties, its fish-full seas, its peaks and its deserts, its flowery landscapes, beaches, islands, trees and treasures, with its huge and long-abandoned factories buried underground making the finest woollen cloths and the brightest silks for them alone.

They knew countless joys. They let themselves be swept along by galloping wild horses, through the long grass of great storm-tossed pampas. They climbed the highest mountains. Wearing skis, they swept down steep slopes dotted with enormous pine trees. They swam in glassy lakes. They marched in the driving rain, breathing in the smell of wet grass. They lay out in the sun. From an outcrop they saw hillocks covered in the flowers of the field. They walked through unsignposted forests. They made love in rooms thick with shade, thickly carpeted, on deep settees.

Then they dreamed of exquisite porcelain decorated with tropical birds, of leather-bound books printed in elzevier on hand-made Japanese vellum, with wide white margins and rough edges on which the eye could rest, of mahogany tables, of supple, comfortable, colourful silk or linen clothing, of bright and spacious rooms, of armfuls of flowers, of Bokhara rugs, of bouncing Dobermanns.

*

Their bodies, their movements were of infinite beauty, their eyes were serene, their hearts transparent, their smiles unruffled.

And in a short-lived apotheosis they saw gigantic palaces built from scratch. On levelled terrain thousands of bonfires were lit, millions of men came to sing *The Messiah*. On vast scaffolds, ten thousand brasses played Verdi's *Requiem*. Poems were picked out on mountainsides. Gardens sprang up in the desert. Whole towns were nothing but frescoes.

But these glittering visions, all these visions which came surging and rushing towards them, which flowed in unstoppable bursts, these vertiginous images of speed, light and triumph, seemed to them at first to be connected to each other in a surprisingly necessary sequence, in an unbounded harmony. It was as if before their bedazzled eyes a finished landscape had suddenly risen up, a total picture of the world, a coherent structure which they could at last grasp and decipher. At first it felt as if their sensations were multiplied by ten, as if their faculties of sight and sense had been amplified to infinite powers, as if a magical bliss accompanied their smallest gesture, kept in time with their steps, suffused their lives: the world was coming towards them, they were going towards the world, they would go on and on discovering it. Their lives were love and ecstasy. Their passion knew no bounds; their freedom was without constraint.

But they were choking under the mass of detail. The visions blurred, became jumbles; they could retain only a few vague and muddled bits, tenuous, persistent, brainless, impoverished wisps. It was not a serene unity, but a brittle fragmentation, as if these visions had only ever been very distant and incalculably darkened reflections, illusory and

93

allusive glimmerings fading away almost as soon as they were born, mere specks of dust: just the banal projection of their clumsiest desires, an almost insubstantial haze of paltry splendours, scraps of dreams they would never be able to grasp.

They thought it was happiness they were inventing in their dreams. They thought their imagination was unshackled, splendid and, with each successive wave, permeated the whole world. They thought that all they had to do was to walk for their stride to be a felicity. But what they were, when they came down to it, was alone, stationary and a bit hollow. A grey and icy flatland, infertile tundra. There was no palace at the desert gate, no esplanade for their horizon.

And from that desperate kind of quest, from that magical feeling of having for an instant almost been able to make it out, albeit dimly, from that extraordinary voyage, from that huge, stationary conquest, from those new-found vistas and those pleasures foretold, from all that was not perhaps impossible beneath their imperfect dream and their admittedly awkward and hobbled impetus which was nonetheless charged (perhaps to the point of inexpressibility) with new emotions and new needs, from all this, nothing remained. They were opening their eyes, hearing the sound of their own voices again, with the muddled mumbling of the man they were interviewing and the hum of the tape-recorder. They could see beside a gun-rack stacked with the shiny butts and gleaming barrels of five sporting rifles, right in front of them, the multicoloured jigsaw puzzle of a land registry chart, and at its centre they could pick out, almost without any astonishment, the nearly complete rectangle of the farmhouse buildings, the grey edging on the track, the quincunx dots marking the plane trees, the heavier lines indicating the main road.

Later on, they were themselves on the grey track lined

with plane trees. They were themselves the little passing glint on the long black road. They were a tiny blot of poverty on the great sea of plenty. They looked around at the great yellow fields with their little red splashes of poppies. And they felt crushed.

PART TWO

I

They tried to run away.

You cannot live in a frenzy for very long. In a world which promised so much and delivered nothing, the tension was too great. They ran out of patience. They realised, one day, or so they thought, that they had to have a place to escape to.

Their lives in Paris were treading water. They had stopped advancing. And on occasions they could see themselves – outdoing each other in the abundance of mistaken details characteristic of all their dreams – as forty-year-old *petits-bourgeois*, with Jérôme running a team of hawkers (Family Protection, Soap for the Blind, Students in Need) and Sylvie keeping house, in a tidy little flat, with a small car, the same little family hotel where they would spend every holiday, and their television set. Or else, at the other extreme, which was far worse, as ageing Bohemians in polo-necks and cord trousers, sitting every evening on the same café terrace in Saint-Germain or Montparnasse, scraping a living from occasional bargains and deals, misers to the tips of their dirty fingernails.

They dreamed of living in the countryside, out of temptation's way. They would lead a calm and frugal life. They would have a white stone house, on the edge of a village, warm elephant-cord trousers, heavy shoes, anoraks, metal-tipped walking sticks and hats, and every day they would go for long walks in the forest. Then they would come back home, would make tea and toast, like the English do, put big logs on the hearth; they would play a quartet on the gramophone, which they would never tire of hearing, would read the great novels they had never had time to read, would have their friends to stay.

Such flights of rural fancy were frequent but rarely got to the point of being actual plans. On two or three occasions, to be fair, they did wonder what kinds of livelihood they might find in the country: there were none. The idea of becoming primary school teachers did occur to them once, but they found it immediately unappealing as they thought of crammed classrooms and days full of stress. They talked vaguely of becoming travelling booksellers, or of going off to an abandoned Provençal *mas* to make rustic pottery. Then they indulged in imagining that they would live in Paris for just three days a week, earning enough to live on comfortably for the rest of their time, which they would spend in the Department of Yonne or Loiret. But these embryonic departures never went very far. They never considered what was really possible, or rather, really impossible, about them.

They dreamed of giving up their jobs, letting go of everything, casting off on a new adventure. They dreamed of starting up again from scratch, of having another go, differently. They were dreaming of a clean break, of saying farewell.

The idea, all the same, was working away and taking root inside them. By mid-September 1962, on their return from a gloomy holiday spoiled by rain and running short of money, they seemed to have made up their minds. An advertisement in *Le Monde* in the first days of October offered teaching jobs in Tunisia. It was not the ideal opportunity – they had dreamed of India, America, Mexico. It was an unglittering, down-to-earth offer, promising neither great fortune nor great adventure. They felt untempted. But they had a few friends in Tunis, old friends from school and college, and then there was the sun, the blue Mediterranean Sea, the promise of a different life, of a real departure, of a different kind of work. They agreed to apply. They were accepted.

Real departures are prepared long in advance. This one was messy. It was more like running away. They spent a fortnight rushing from office to office for medical certificates, for passports, for visas, for tickets, for luggage. Then four days before they were due to leave they learned that Sylvie, who had completed two years of her degree course, had been appointed to the Technical College at Sfax, one hundred and seventy miles from Tunis, whereas Jérôme, who had only a first-year pass by way of qualification, had been given a primary-school job at Mahares, twenty-three miles in the other direction.

It was bad news. They wanted to back out. Tunis, where accommodation had been booked for them, where they were expected, was where they had wanted to go, where they thought they were going. But it was too late. They had sub-let their flat, booked their seats, given their farewell party. They had been getting ready to go for a long time. And then Sfax, of which they had barely heard the name before, was at the end of the world, a desert, and, with their pronounced inclination for extremes, they even began to take pleasure in thinking that they were going to be cut off from everything, remote from everything, isolated as they never had been before. However, they agreed that a primary school post was, if not too much of a slide, at least too heavy a burden: Jérôme succeeded in having his contract cancelled: one salary would be enough to live on until he could find some sort of work on the spot.

And so they left. They were seen to the station, and, on the morning of 23 October, with four trunks full of books and a camp bed, they boarded the *Commandant-Crubellier* at Marseilles, bound for Tunis. The crossing was bad and the dinner was not good. They were sea-sick, took pills and slept soundly. In the morning Tunisia was in sight. It was a fine day. They smiled to each other. They saw an island which they were told was called *Ile Plane*, then great long and narrow beaches, and, after they had passed La Goulette and entered the Lake of Tunis, flocks of migrating birds.

They were happy to have left. They felt they were emerging from a hell of crowded metro carriages, insufficient sleep, aching teeth and uncertainty. Their minds were clouded. Their life had been only a kind of endless tightrope walk leading nowhere: empty appetite, naked desire without bounds or props. They felt exhausted. They had left to go to ground, to forget, to wind down.

The sun shone. The boat moved slowly, silently, along the narrow channel. On the road quite close to them, people stood in open-topped cars and waved vigorously at them. In the sky there were little white clouds standing still. It was already hot. The panels beneath the handrail were warm to the touch. On the deck below them, sailors were stacking up deckchairs, rolling up the long tarpaulins which covered the holds. Queues lined up at the gangways for disembarkation.

They got to Sfax two days later, towards two in the afternoon, after a seven-hour train journey. The heat was overpowering. Opposite the tiny white and pink station building there lay an endless avenue grey with dust, lined with ugly palms and new-built blocks. A few minutes after the train had come in, after the sparse cars and bicycles had left, the town returned to a state of total silence.

They left their cases in left luggage. They went down the avenue, which was called Avenue Bourguiba. After about three hundred yards they came upon a restaurant. A sizable wall-mounted adjustable ventilator hummed jerkily. On greasy tables with oil-cloth tablecloths a few dozen flies had congregated; a stubble-chinned waiter nonchalantly flicked them away with a napkin. For two hundred francs they had a meal of tuna salad and veal cutlet.

Then they looked for a hotel, booked a room, had their cases brought over. They washed their hands and faces, lay down for a moment, changed, and went back down. Sylvie went to the Technical College, Jérôme waited outside on a bench. Towards four o'clock, Sfax began slowly to reawaken. Hundreds of children appeared, then veiled women, policemen dressed in grey poplin, beggars, carts, donkeys, spotless *bourgeois*.

Sylvie emerged with her timetable in her hand. They carried on walking. They drank a can of beer and ate olives and salted almonds. Barkers were selling the day before yesterday's *Figaro*. They had arrived.

The next day Sylvie made the acquaintance of some of her new colleagues, who helped them find a flat. It consisted of three huge rooms with high ceilings and was absolutely bare: a long passageway led to a small square room from which five doors opened, three of them to the bedrooms, one to a bathroom and one to a vast kitchen. Two balconies looked out onto a small fishing harbour, south channel A dock, which offered some resemblance to Saint-Tropez, and onto a foul-smelling lagoon. They took their first steps in the Arab quarter, bought a metal bedstead, a horse-hair mattress, two cane chairs, four rope stools, two tables, a thick yellow raffia mat with sparse decorations in red.

Then Sylvie began teaching. Day by day they settled in. Their trunks, which had been shipped as freight, arrived. They unpacked books, records, the record-player, the trinkets. With large sheets of red, grey and green blotting paper they made lampshades. They bought long planks of barely planed wood and twelve-hole bricks, and they covered two-thirds of the walls with bookshelves. On all the walls they stuck dozens of reproductions and on a prominently-positioned wallboard they pinned photographs of all their friends.

It was a cold and dismal dwelling. With its too-high walls painted with a brownish sort of yellow distemper which kept flaking off in large pieces, with its large, uniform, colourless tiles on all the floors, with its unusable volume, the flat was altogether too big and too bare for them to be able to live in it. There would have had to be five or six of them, a group of good friends drinking, eating, talking. But they were on their own, and lost. The living room, containing the camp bed on which they had put a small mattress and a colourful bedspread, the thick raffia mat strewn with a few cushions, and, above all, the books (the row of collected works in the Pléiade editions, the run of periodicals, the four Tisné volumes), the trinkets, the records, the large mariner's chart, *The Great Parade*, all the things which not so long ago had constituted the decor of their other life, all the things which took them back from this universe of sand and stone to Rue de Quatrefages, to the tree that stayed green for so long, to the little gardens – the living room, at least, still exuded a little warmth. Lying flat on the mat, with a tiny cup of Turkish coffee at their sides, they would listen to the *Kreutzer Sonata*, the *Archduke*, *Death and the Maiden*, and it was as though the music (which in this large and sparsely furnished room, almost as large as a hall, acquired stunning acoustics) came to inhabit it, and all of a sudden transformed it: like a guest, a very dear friend who had been lost sight of and found again by chance, coming to share their meal, talking to them of Paris. On a cool November evening, in this foreign city where nothing was theirs, where they were ill at ease, music took them backwards, allowed them to recover an almost forgotten feeling of complicity and shared living, as if, inside a tiny island – within the boundaries of the mat, the two sets of shelving, the record-player, the circle of light confined by the cylindrical lampshade – they had managed to establish and to preserve a protected area which time and space could not touch. But outside, all around, was exile and the unknown: the long passageway where footsteps echoed too loudly, the vast, icy, hostile bedroom with only a wide, too-hard bed smelling of straw for furniture and an unstable lamp on an old tea-chest which did as a bedside table, a wicker trunk full of dirty washing, a stool littered with clothes; and the third room, not used, where they never went. Then the stone staircase, the main foyer perpetually threatened by the sand; the street: three two-storey blocks of flats, a shed where sponges were dried, a plot of waste ground; the town around.

In Sfax they spent what were probably the queerest eight months of their lives.

The port and the European quarter of Sfax had been destroyed during the war, and the city now consisted of about thirty streets set at right angles to each other. The two main streets were Avenue Bourguiba, running from the station to the Central Market, near where they lived, and Avenue Hedi-Chaker, which ran from the port to the Arab quarter. The city centre was the intersection of these two streets: that was where the town hall was to be found, with two of its ground-floor rooms containing a few ancient ceramics and half a dozen mosaics, as well as the statue and tomb of Hedi Chaker, murdered by the Main Rouge terrorists shortly before independence, the *Café de Tunis*, frequented by Arabs and the *Café de la Régence*, frequented by Europeans, a little flowerbed, a news-stand and a tobacconist's.

Just over fifteen minutes was enough to go right round the European quarter. From the building they lived in, the Technical College was three minutes' walk away, the market was two minutes away, the restaurant where they ate all their meals was five minutes away and the *Café de la Régence* took six minutes to reach, as did the bank, the municipal library and six of the city's seven cinemas. The post office, the station and the hire point for cars to Tunis and Gabès were less than ten minutes' walk and constituted the outer limits of sufficient knowledge for living in Sfax.

The Arab quarter, an ancient, beautiful, fortified city, displayed grey-brown walls and gates which were justifiably considered admirable. They often entered the Arab quarter, made it almost the only goal of all their walks, but because they were indeed only walking through, they remained for ever strangers in it. They did not understand its basic mechanisms, all they could see was a labyrinth of alleys. Raising their eyes, they might admire a wrought-iron balcony, a painted beam-end, the pure ogive arch of a window, the subtle play of light and shade, an extremely narrow staircase – but their walks had no aim. They turned around on themselves, always afraid of getting lost, tiring easily. In the end there was nothing to attract them in this sequence of poverty-stricken stalls, of almost identical shops, of cramped bazaars, in this incomprehensible alternation of crowded and deserted streets, in this throng which did not seem to be going anywhere at all.

Such feelings of foreignness grew all the more marked, became almost oppressive when, faced with long empty afternoons and desperate Sundays, they crossed right through the Arab quarter and, beyond Bab Djebli, got as far as the endless suburbs of Sfax. Stretching out for miles were tiny garden plots, hedges of prickly pear, wattle-and-daub houses, huts made of corrugated iron and cardboard boxes; and then huge abandoned and rotting pools, and, far away, at the vanishing point of the horizon, the first olive groves. They would loiter for hours on end; they would wander past barracks, cross waste ground and derelict quagmires.

And when they returned to the European quarter, when they passed in front of the Hillal or the Nour cinema, when they sat down at the *Régence* and clapped their hands to call the waiter, ordered a Coca-Cola or a can of beer, bought the latest issue of *Le Monde*, whistled for the hawker, dressed as always in his long, dirty, white smock and his canvas skullcap, to buy a few twists of peanuts, grilled almonds, pistachios and pine-nuts, only then did they know that melancholy feeling that this was their home.

They would walk beside palm trees grey with dust; they would pass along in front of the neo-Moorish façades of Avenue Bourguiba; they would cast vague glances at hideous window-displays: flimsy furniture, wrought-iron standard lamps, electric blankets, school exercise books, evening dress, ladies' shoes, bottled gas canisters. It was the only world they had, their real world. They dragged their feet on the way back; Jérôme would make coffee in *zazouas* made in Czechoslovakia; Sylvie corrected a pile of homework.

To begin with Jérôme had tried to find work. He went to Tunis several times and, thanks to some letters of introduction he had had written before leaving France and to the contacts of his Tunisian friends, he met some functionaries at the Ministry of Information, in broadcasting, in tourism and in the Education Service. It was a waste of time. Market research did not exist in Tunisia, nor did part-time jobs, and the few sinecures that existed were fully occupied. He had no qualifications. He was neither an engineer, nor an accountant, nor a draughtsman, nor a doctor. He was again offered a teaching job; he wasn't keen; very soon he gave up all hope. Sylvie's salary allowed them to live modestly; in Sfax that was the commonest kind of living.

Sylvie wore herself out trying to instill, as the syllabus required, the hidden beauties of Malherbe and Racine in pupils who were older than she was and didn't know how to write. Jérôme wasted his time. He started off on various projects – taking a diploma in sociology, sorting out his ideas about film – which he couldn't keep up. He wandered around the streets in his Weston shoes, strolled up and down the port, sauntered through the market. He went to the museum, exchanged a few words with the duty guard, spent a few minutes looking at an ancient amphora, a funeral inscription or a mosaic: Daniel in the Lions' Den, Amphitrite astride a dolphin. He went to watch a tennis match on the courts laid out beneath the ramparts, he walked through the Arab quarter, loitered in the bazaars, weighing up fabrics, copperware, saddles. He bought all the newspapers, did the crosswords, borrowed books from the library, wrote rather dismal letters to his friends, who often did not reply.

Sylvie's job timetabled their lives. Their week was made of good days – Mondays, because they had the morning off and because the cinemas changed their films; Wednesdays, because they had a free afternoon; and Fridays, because they had the whole day off and, once again, the films changed – and bad days: all the rest. Sunday was an intermediate day, pleasant in the morning (they would stay in bed, the Paris weeklies would come), boring in the afternoon, gloomy in the evening unless, by chance, there was a film to attract them, but it was not often that two notable or even just watchable films were put on in the same half-week. And so the weeks passed. They followed each other with mechanical regularity: four weeks to a month, more or less; the months were all the same. The days, after getting shorter and shorter, began to get longer and longer. The winter was wet, almost cold. Their lives were dripping away.

II

They were absolutely alone.

Sfax was an inscrutable city. They felt, on occasions, that no-one would ever find out how to pierce its mystery. Its doors would never open. There were people in the street, in the evenings, in self-contained crowds, people coming and going, an almost continuous tide of them under the awnings of Avenue Hedi-Chaker, in front of the *Mabrouk Hotel*, the Destour Information Office, the Hillal cinema, the cake-shop called *Les Délices*; there were public places – cafés, restaurants, cinemas – almost crammed with people; and faces which, now and again, might almost seem familiar. But all around, on the quayside, on the ramparts, as soon as you got away from the centre, it was a void, it was dead: the huge sand-strewn esplanade in front of Sfax's hideous cathedral encircled by dwarf palms, Boulevard de Picville, lined by waste plots and two-storey maisonettes, Rue Mangolte, Rue Fezzani, Rue Abd-el-Kader Zghal were bare, straight and sand-swept. Sickly palm-trees swayed before the wind; from their trunks erupting in woody bracts barely a handful of fronds emerged. A multitude of cats prowled amongst the dustbins. A yellow-coated dog sometimes scuttled past with its tail between its legs.

Not a soul stirring. Behind ever-bolted doors, only bare passageways, stone stairs, windowless courtyards. Streets upon streets set at right angles to each other, metal roller-blinds, high wooden fences, a world of squares that were not squares, of non-streets, of phantom avenues. They would walk, not speaking, disoriented; and sometimes it seemed that everything was but an illusion, that Sfax did not exist, did not breathe. They sought signs of complicity all around. Nothing answered their call. They felt isolated in a way that was almost painful. They had been dispossessed, the world was no longer for swimming in, no longer in their arms, and never would be. It was as if, long ago and once and for all, an order had been made, a strict rule had been established to cut them out: they would be free to wander where they willed without let or hindrance, without anyone speaking to them. They would be for ever incognito, for ever strangers in the land. The Italians, the Maltese and the Greeks in the port would watch them go by and stay silent. Olive-oil entrepreneurs in their all-white garb and gold-rimmed glasses, passing slowly by on Rue du Bey with a beadle in their train, would walk straight past without seeing them.

Sylvie's colleagues at work provided only distant and often stand-offish relationships. French teachers with permanent posts did not seem to have unalloyed esteem for temporary staff. Even those who were not bothered by this distinction found it hard to forgive Sylvie for not being made in their own image. She should have been a teacher's wife as well as a career teacher herself, and a regular small-town, middle-class housewife, and have some dignity, deportment, culture. Not let the old country down, don't you know. And though there were in a sense two classes of expatriates – teachers at the start of their careers, eager to grab a suburban semi as fast as they could in Angoulême, Béziers or Tarbes, and the cohort of conscientious objectors or disciplinary cases who did not get the colonial service bonus in their pay but could afford to despise the first group (but the latter were a dying breed: most objectors had been pardoned; others were leaving to settle in Algeria or French Guinea) – neither class was prepared, apparently, to concede that you could sit in the cinema in the front row, next to native ragamuffins, or saunter unshaven, unbuttoned, in the street, in clogs, like a ne'er-do-well. A few books were swapped, and a few records; there was the odd discussion at *La Régence*; and that was that. No warm hospitality, no keen friendship. That wasn't a plant that grew in Sfax. People turned in on themselves, in their houses that were too big for them.

With other groups – with the French staff at the Sfax-Gafsa Company or the *Compagnie des Pétroles*, with Muslims, with Jews, with *pieds-noirs* settlers – it was even worse: no contact at all was possible. Sometimes they would go for a whole week without speaking to anyone.

It soon occurred to them that they were going to stop living altogether. Time passed and stood still. There was no longer anything to keep them in touch with the world, apart from eternally out-of-date newspapers which they began to suspect were well-meaning fabrications, or the memories of anterior life, shadows of another world. They had always lived in Sfax, they would always live there. They had lost all their plans, all their impatience. They looked forward to nothing, not even to holidays too far over the horizon, not even to returning to France.

They felt neither joy, nor sadness, nor even boredom, but they did wonder sometimes if they still existed, if they really existed. They drew no special satisfaction from asking this deceptive question, beyond this: on occasions, it seemed to them, in a muddled and murky way, that the life they were leading was appropriate, adequate and, paradoxically, necessary. They were in the centre of a vacuum, they had settled into a no man's land of parallel streets, yellow sand, inlets and dusty palm-trees, a world they did not understand, that they did not seek to understand, because, in their past lives, they had never equipped themselves to have to adapt, one day, to change, to mould themselves to a different kind of scenery, or climate, or style of living. Sylvie did not resemble even for an instant the teacher she was supposed to be, and Jérôme, as he traipsed down the street, could easily seem to have brought his homeland, or rather his *quartier*, his ghetto, his stamping-ground, with him on the soles of his English shoes. But Rue Larbi-Zarouk, where they had built their nest, did not even have the mosque which ennobles Rue de Quatrefages, and as for the rest, despite their occasionally strenuous efforts to summon it all up in their imagination, Sfax simply did not have a MacMahon, or a *Harry's Bar*, or a *Balzar*, or a Contrescarpe, or a Salle Pleyel, or *Berges de la Seine une nuit de juin*. In such a vacuum, precisely because of this vacuum, because of the absence of all things, because of such a fundamental vacuity, such a blank zone, a *tabula rasa*, they felt as if they were being cleansed, returning to a greater simplicity, to true modesty. And in a place as poor as Tunisia, to tell the truth, their own financial straits, the petty poverty of civilised people accustomed to showers, cars and cold drinks, did not mean very much.

Sylvie took her classes, tested her pupils, marked her scripts. Jérôme went to the City Library, read books at random: Borges, Troyat, Zeraffa. They ate in a little restaurant, almost always at the same table. Tuna salad, veal cutlet, or a kebab, or lemon sole, fruit. They went to *La Régence* for an espresso served with a glass of cold water. They read heaps of newspapers, saw films, loitered in the streets.

Their life was like an unrelinquished habit, an almost unruffled tedium: a life sans everything.

III

From April, they began to travel a little. On occasions when they had three or four days free and were not too short of money, they hired a car and drove towards the South. Alternatively, on Saturdays at six in the evening, a taxi-bus would take them off to Susa or Tunis until Monday at noon.

They tried to get away from Sfax, from its dreary streets and emptiness, so as to find vistas, sights and ruins which perhaps would dazzle or bowl them over, some glowing marvel which would even the score. The remains of a palace, or a temple, or an amphitheatre, a verdant oasis seen from a peak near Kairouan, a long strip of fine sand forming a curved beach as far as the eye could see, sometimes rewarded their search. But more often they escaped from Sfax only to find, a few dozen or a few hundred miles further on, identically dreary streets, identically incomprehensible and bustling bazaars, identical inlets and ugly palms, an identical desert.

They saw Gabes, Tuzer, Nefta, Gafsa and Metlaoui; the ruins of Sbeitla, Kasserine and Thelepte; they passed through dead towns with names which had previously sounded to their ears like magic: Mahares, Moulares, Matmata, Medenin; they pushed on to the Libyan border.

For miles and miles, the land was stony, dusty, uninhabitable. Nothing grew, bar a few clumps of almost yellow, razor-sharp grass. It felt as if they had been driving for hours on end in a pall of dust, along a road marked out only by old ruts or faded tyre-tracks, into a horizon of nothing but dumpy, dun-coloured hills, without coming across anything at all apart from a dead donkey, a rusted jerrycan, a half-collapsed pile of stones which had perhaps been a house.

Or else they would follow a signposted but pot-holed and occasionally almost dangerous road across enormous shatts, and, on every side, as far as the eye could see, there would be nothing but a whitish crust glaring in the sun and throwing up on the horizon sudden flashes which, now and then, seemed almost like mirages, the sea breaking, battlements. They would stop the car and walk a few steps. Beneath the crust of salt, lumps of dry and fissured light brown clay would sometimes collapse and expose blacker areas of compressed and spongy mud which you risked sinking into, almost.

Mangy camels entangled on their tethers as they ripped leaves off an oddly twisted tree with violent swipes of their heads and then jutted their stupid blubber lips out at the road; distempered dogs, half wild, running round in circles; shattered dry-stone walls; black long-haired goats; low tents made of patchworks of pieces of blanket: these were the signs of an approaching village or town, consisting of a long line of rectangular, single-storey houses with dirty white walls, a square minaret and a domed shrine. They overtook a peasant jogging alongside his donkey, and stopped at the sole hotel.

Three men squatting with their backs to the wall were eating bread dipped in oil. Children were running. A woman entirely draped in a black or purple veil which covered her eyes as well would sometimes be seen slipping from one house to another. The terraces of the two cafés spilled out a long way into the street. A tannoy broadcast Arab music, grating melodies played on rasping zithers, jangling timbrels, a flute playing a piercing dirge, refrains which were modulated, reprised, then done in unison, da capo, a hundred times over. Men, sitting in the shade, drinking tea in small glasses, played dominoes.

They went past huge water tanks, along a poorly-made track, and came upon the ruins: four pillars twenty feet tall with nothing to support any more, wrecked buildings whose ground plan had been preserved by the imprints in the earth of the floor-tiling in each room, by isolated steps, cellars, paved streets, remnants of sewers. And people claiming to be guides offered to sell them little silver fish, shiny coins, terracotta figurines.

Then, before leaving, they would go to the market, into the bazaar. They would get lost in the labyrinth of arcades, dead ends, and passageways. A barber would be shaving someone in the open, beside a huge heap of gugglets. A donkey would be burdened with two conical hampers of plaited rope brim-full of ground pimento. In the jewellers' souk, in the textile souk, tradesmen sitting cross-legged, unshod, on a pile of blankets, would roll out piled carpets and fustian in front of them, offer them red woollen burnouses, haicks of wool and silk, leather saddles embroidered with silver thread, beaten brass trays, fretwork boxes, guns, musical instruments, small jewels, scarves with gold thread drawn through, and parchments adorned with bold arabesques.

They bought nothing. Obviously, to some degree, because they did not know how to buy and were worried about having to haggle, but above all because they did not feel drawn to these things. None of them, however lavish they could occasionally be, gave them a feeling of wealth. They moved on, amused or indifferent, but all they saw remained foreign, belonged to another world, did not concern them. And from these trips they brought back only images of emptiness and drought: desolate heaths, tundra, sea inlets, a mineral world where nothing grows: their own world of loneliness, their own dry desert.

It was in Tunisia, all the same, that one day they saw the house of their dreams, the most beautiful dwelling imaginable. It was the house, at Hammamet, of an ageing English couple who divided their time between Tunisia and Florence and for whom hospitality seemed to have become their only recourse against dying from mutual boredom. There were at least a dozen other house guests at the same time as Jérôme and Sylvie. The atmosphere was one of futility, often to the point of exasperation: parlour games, bridge and canasta took turns in between somewhat snooty conversations in which not entirely out-dated gossip coming direct from the capitals of Europe gave rise to informed and often firm-minded judgments (I like the man very much and what he's doing is quite right . . .).

But the house was paradise on earth. Set in the midst of a great park sloping gently down to a fine sandy beach, it was an old building in the local idiom, not particularly large, all on one level, which had grown year by year and become the sun of a whole constellation of pavilions of all sizes, of arbours, shrines, bungalows with verandas on all four sides, dotted around the estate and connected to each other by lattice-walled walkways. There was an octagonal room with no openings other than a small door and two narrow slit windows, with its thick walls entirely lined with books, which was as shady and cool as a tomb; there were tiny rooms, whitewashed like monastic cells, with only two Saharan armchairs and a low table to furnish them; other rooms were long, low and narrow, with walls hung with thick mats, and yet others furnished in English country style, with inglenooks and massive fireplaces flanked by a pair of settees facing each other. In the grounds, white marble-paved paths meandered amongst the lemon trees, the orange trees and the almonds, lined with fragments of antique pillars. There were brooks and waterfalls, grottos and ponds covered with large white water-lilies between which you could sometimes see the silvery streak of fish. Peacocks paraded, uncaged, just as they had dreamed. Bowers overgrown with roses led to lush hideaways.

But it was probably too late. The three days they spent at Hammamet did not shake off their torpor. For them, it was as if all this luxury and comfort, this profusion of things offered with their immediately obvious beauty concerned them no longer. In times past they would have gone to hell to have the hand-painted tiles they saw in the bathroom, for the fountains in the grounds, for the tartan carpet in the main hall, for the library's oak panelling, for the china, the vases, the rugs. They acknowledged them as memories; they had not become insensitive to them, but they no longer understood them; all their landmarks were missing. That was certainly the Tunisia they would have found it easiest to settle in, cosmopolitan Tunisia with its remnants of prestige, pleasant climate and its colourful and picturesque life. That was certainly the kind of life they had first dreamed of: but they had turned into Sfaxians, provincials, exiles.

A world without memories, without memory. More time passed, days and weeks of desert waste, which did not count. They had stopped wanting. An indifferent world. Trains came, ships docked, unloaded machine-tools, medicines, ball-bearings, took on phosphates and olive-oil. Lorries loaded with straw crossed the town on their way to the South, where there was famine. Their life went on identically: teaching, espressos at *La Régence*, old films in the evening, newspapers, crosswords. They were walking in their sleep. They no longer knew what they wanted. They were dispossessed.

It now seemed to them that before – and each day, that *before* receded further into the past, as if their anterior life was falling slowly into the domain of legend, of the unreal, or of the shapeless – before, they had had at least a passion for possessing. Often it was wanting that had been all their existence. They had felt drawn towards the future, impatient, consumed with desire.

And then what? What had they done? What had happened?

Something resembling a quiet and very gentle tragedy was entering the heart of their decelerating lives. They were adrift in the rubble of a very ancient dream, lost amidst unrecognisable ruins.

There was nothing left. They were at the finishing line, at the terminus of the doubtful trajectory which had been their life for six years, at the end of that uncertain quest which had taken them nowhere, which had taught them nothing.

Epilogue

Things could have carried on in the same way. They could have stayed like that all their lives. Jérôme would have got a job for himself. They would not have been short of money. They would have got transferred to Tunis eventually. They would have made new friends. They would have bought themselves a car. At La Marsa, or Sidibou Saïd, or El Manza, they would have had a fine detached house, a big garden.

But it will not be easy for them to escape from their own story. Time once again will work in their stead. The school year will come to an end. It will turn deliciously hot. Jérôme will spend his days on the beach and Sylvie will come to join him when her classes are over. There will be the last scripts to mark. They will feel holidays coming on. They will pine for Paris, for spring on the banks of the Seine, for their tree all in flower, for the Champs-Elysées, for Place des Vosges. Their eyes will water as they reminisce over their dearly-cherished freedom, their lazy mornings, their candle-lit dinners. And friends will send them their holiday plans: a big house in Touraine, good food, outings in the country: "What if . . . we went back?" one of them will say.

"It could all be just like it used to be," the other will answer.

They will pack. They will sort the books, the prints, the

snapshots of their friends, they will throw away huge quantities of paperwork, give away their furniture, their poorly planed planks, their twelve-hole bricks, and ship their trunks. They will count the days, the hours, the minutes.

Their last hours in Sfax will be spent on a solemn repetition of their ritual walk. They will cross the central market, pass by the port for a bit, admire as they do every day the huge natural sponges drying in the sun, go past the Italian delicatessen, the *Hôtel des Oliviers*, past the City Library and then, turning back on themselves down Avenue Bourguiba, they will skirt the hideous cathedral and fork off at the Collège where for the last time they will nod, as they nod every day, to Monsieur Michri, the chief caretaker, who will be plodding up and down in front of the gates, then go along Rue Victor-Hugo, take one last look at their regular restaurant, at the Greek church. Then they will enter the Arab quarter by the Kasbah gate, take Rue Bab Djedid, then Rue du Bey, emerging by the Bab Diwan gate to reach the awnings of Avenue Hedi-Chaker, and on past the theatre, the two cinemas, the bank, before drinking their last cup of coffee at *La Régence*, buying their last cigarettes, their last newspaper.

Two minutes later they will take their seats in a hired Peugeot 403 about to depart. Their cases will have been roped to the roof-rack long before. They will clutch their wallets to their chests, their boarding passes, their rail tickets, their luggage receipts.

The car will move off slowly. At half-past five of a summer's evening, Sfax will be a truly beautiful city. Its pristine buildings will glisten in the sunlight. The towers and crenellated ramparts of the Arab quarter will rise up in pride. Boy Scouts all dressed up in red and white will march by in step. Tunisian flags, a white crescent on a red ground, and the green-and-red ensign of Algeria, will wave in the breeze.

There will be a bit of the sea, so blue, then big building sites, interminable suburbs jammed with donkeys, children and bicycles, then the endless olive groves. And then the open road: Sakietes-Zit, El Djem and its amphitheatre, Msaken the city of brigands, Susa and its overpopulated sea-front, Enfidaville and its huge olive plantations, Bir bou Rekba and its coffee shops, fruit and ceramics, Grombalia, Potinville and its vine-covered hills, Hammam Lif, then a stretch of motorway, industrial suburbs, soap factories, cement works: Tunis.

They will spend hours swimming at Carthage, amidst the ruins, at La Marsa; they will go all the way to Utica, to Kelibia, to Nabeul, where they will buy a gugglet, to Goletta where, late in the evening, they will eat amazing bream.

Then one day at six in the morning they will be at the docks. Embarkation procedures will be long and tiresome; they will struggle to find a place on deck to pitch their chairs.

The crossing will be uneventful. At Marseilles they will drink a bowl of *café au lait* with croissants. They will buy yesterday's *Le Monde* and *Libération*. On the train they will hear the wheels beating out the bars of songs of victory, of the Hallelujah chorus, of triumphant hymns. They will count the kilometres; they will be in raptures over the French countryside, its great wheatfields, its green forests, its pastures and gentle rolling hills.

They will get in at eleven in the evening. All their friends will be at the station. They will be amazed at how well they look: they will be as tanned as trekkers, and wearing broad-brimmed hats of plaited straw. They will tell all about Sfax, deserts, splendid ruins, how cheaply you can live there, the sea so blue. They will be dragged off to "Harry's". They will get drunk straight away. They will be happy.

And so they will return, and it will be even worse. Rue de Quatrefages will still be there, with its wonderful tree, and their little flat, so quaint, with its low ceiling, with its one red-curtained window and its one green-curtained window, its good old books, its heaps of newspapers, its narrow bed, its tiny kitchen, its mess.

They will see Paris again, and it will be all that life can afford. They will saunter by the banks of the Seine, in the gardens of Palais-Royal, in the side-streets of Saint-Germain. And every night, in the brightly-lit streets, every shop window will once again be a wondrous enticement. Stalls will groan with the weight of foodstuffs. They will join in the shoving throng in department stores. They will thrust their hands into folds of silk, cup their hands around chunky phials of perfume, brush their hands over ties.

They will try to live as they lived before. They will pick up their old contacts in the agencies. But the spells will have broken. Once again they will suffocate. They will think they are dying from things being too small, too cramped.

They will dream of fortune. They will look in the gutters in the hope of coming across a bulging wallet, a bank note, a franc, a metro ticket.

They will dream of getting away to the country. They will dream of Sfax.

They won't stick it out for long.

And so one day – had they not always known that this day would come? – they will decide to be done with it, once and for all, like everyone else. Their friends, in the know, will look out for jobs for them. A good word will be put in at several agencies. Full of hope, they will write carefully pondered curricula vitae. Their luck – but it will not be luck exactly – will be in. Their employment records, despite being irregular, will be given particular scrutiny. They will be summoned. They will manage to find the words that are needed to make a good impression.

And that is how after a few years of errant living, weary of not having enough money, weary of counting the pennies and of resenting the counting, Jérôme and Sylvie will accept – perhaps with thanks – twin executive posts accompanied by salaries which could just about pass for a golden hello which some big shot will offer them in advertising.

They will go to Bordeaux to take over an agency. They will prepare their departure with care. They will sort out their flat, have it repainted, get rid of the piles of books, the bundles of linen, the stacks of crockery that had always cluttered it up and beneath which they had often felt they were suffocating. They will walk around their almost unrecognisable two-roomed apartment which they had always said it was impossible to do anything in, especially to walk round. They will see it for the first time the way they had always wanted to see it, at last repainted, sparkling white and clean, without a speck of dust, unstained, without a crack in the plaster or a tear in the wallpaper, with its low ceiling, its rustic courtyard, its admirable tree over which, very soon, just as they had in the past, the new owners will fall into raptures.

They will sell their books to dealers and their old rags to second-hand clothes shops. They will do the round of tailor, dressmaker, shirtmaker. They will pack their trunks.

They will not really earn a fortune. They will not be chairmen or managing directors. The only millions they will manipulate will belong to other people. They will get some of the crumbs, for appearances, for silk shirts, for pigskin gloves. They will be presentable. They will be well housed, well fed, well dressed. They will not be wanting.

They will have their chesterfield settee, their armchairs in soft natural leather as stylish as seats in Italian racing cars, their rustic tables, their lecterns, and their fitted carpets, silk rugs, and light oak bookcases.

They will have huge and empty rooms full of light; plenty of clearance, glass panels, magnificent outlook. They will have china, silver cutlery, lace napkins, sumptu ous red leather bindings.

They will not yet be thirty. They will have their whole lives ahead of them.

They will leave Paris early one September. They will be in an almost empty first-class carriage. The train will pick up speed almost straight away. The aluminium carriage will sway comfortingly.

They will leave. They will leave everything behind them. They will run. Nothing could have held them.

"Do you remember?" Jérôme will say. And they will muse on time past, dark days, youth, their first friendships, their first surveys, the tree in the courtyard in Rue de Quatrefages, the friends they had lost, the comradely dinner parties. They will recall how they would cross Paris to look for cigarettes, and stop in front of antique dealers. They will summon up memories of their days in Sfax, their slow death, their almost triumphant return.

"So here we are," Sylvie will say. And it will seem to them to be almost a matter of course.

They will feel at ease in their lightweight clothes. They will spread themselves out in the deserted carriage. The French countryside will march past. They will look in silence on the great fields of ripe wheat, the burnt rigging of the high-tension pylons. They will see glassworks, almost spanking new factories, large holiday camps, dams, small houses all alone in clearings. Children will be running along a white road.

The journey will be pleasant for a long while. Towards noon they will wander nonchalantly down to the dining car. They will sit by a window, facing each other. They will order two whiskies. They will look at each other one last time with a smile of complicity. The starched table linen, the solid cutlery engraved with the arms of the *Compagnie des Wagons-Lits*, the weighty, emblazoned crockery will seem like a prelude to a sumptuous feast. But the meal they will be served will be quite simply tasteless . . .

The means is as much part of the truth as the result. The quest for truth must itself be true; the true quest is the unfurling of a truth whose different parts combine in the result.

KARL MARX

A MAN ASLEEP

Translated from the French by
Andrew Leak

for Paulette
In memoriam J.P.

There is no need for you to leave the house. Stay at your table and listen. Don't even listen, just wait. Don't even wait, be completely quiet and alone. The world will offer itself to you to be unmasked, it can't do otherwise, in raptures it will writhe before you.

FRANZ KAFKA
(Reflections on Sin, Suffering,
Hope, and the True Way)

As soon as you close your eyes, the adventure of sleep begins. The familiar half-light of the bedroom, a dark volume broken by details, where your memory can easily identify the paths your eyes have followed a thousand times (retracing them from the opaque square of the window, eliciting the washbasin from a shaft of reflected light and the shelving from the slightly less dark shadow of a book, distinguishing the blacker mass of the hanging clothes), gives way, after a while, to a two-dimensional space, something like a board of indefinite extension set at a very shallow angle to the plane of your eyes, as if it were propped not quite vertically on the bridge of your nose; the board might at first seem evenly grey, or rather, neutral, that is to say shapeless and colourless, but probably quite quickly turns out to possess at least two properties: the first is that it becomes more or less dark depending on how tightly, or loosely, you screw up your eyes, as if, more precisely, the force brought to bear on your eyebrows when you close your eyes had the effect of altering the angle of the plane in relation to your body, as if it were hinged to your eyebrows, and, consequently, although the only proof of this consequence is the evidence of your own eyes, had the effect also of altering the density, or the quality, of the darkness you perceive; the second property is that the surface of this space is not at all regular, or, more precisely, that the distribution, the allocation, of the areas of darkness is not homogeneous: the upper area is manifestly darker, whereas the lower area, which, to you, appears nearer (although, of course, the notions of proximity and distance, above and below, in front and behind, have already ceased to be altogether precise) is, on the one hand, much greyer, not, that is to say, much more neutral as you initially believe, but actually much whiter, and, on the other hand, contains, or supports, one, two, or several bag-like objects, or capsules, a little how you imagine, for example, a tear gland to be, with thin, ciliated edges, and within which, quivering, twitching, writhing, are some intensely white flashes, some of them extremely thin, like infinitely fine stripes, others much thicker, almost fat, like maggots. These flashes, although 'flashes' is a quite inappropriate term, have a curious quality: they cannot be looked at. As soon as your attention lingers on them too long, and it is virtually impossible to avoid this, since, after all, they are dancing in front of you and all the rest scarcely exists, indeed, all that is really perceptible is the hinge of your eyebrows and the very vague, more or less perceptible two-dimensional space in which the darkness stretches away unevenly, but as soon as you look at them, although this word, of course, no longer means anything, as soon as you attempt, let us say, to satisfy yourself a little as to their form, or their substance, or a detail, you can be sure to find yourself back again, your eyes open, across from the window, itself an opaque rectangle becoming a square again, in spite of the fact that these little bags bear no resemblance to it whatsoever. However, they reappear almost as soon as you close your eyes again, and with them the more or less sloping space hinged to your eyebrows, and, in all likelihood, they haven't changed since the last time. But you cannot be absolutely sure on this last point, for, after an interval of time which it is difficult to estimate, and although nothing enables you to affirm that they have actually disappeared, you are able to note that they have grown considerably paler. Now you are dealing with a kind of streaky grey drizzle, still part of this same space which is an extension more or less of your eyebrows, but distorted, apparently, to the point where it is constantly veering to the left; you can look at it, explore it, without shattering the whole, without causing yourself to wake up immediately, but this is not in the least bit interesting. It is on the right that something is taking place, a plank as it happens, somewhat behind, somewhat above, somewhat to the right. You can't see the plank, obviously. All you know is that it is hard, although you are not on it, since, precisely, you are on something that is very soft, and that something is your body. Then suddenly a truly amazing phenomenon occurs: first, there are three spaces which it is quite impossible to confuse, your body-bed which is soft, horizontal and white, then the bar of your eyebrows which controls a grey, mediocre, slanting space, and finally the plank, which is immobile and very hard on top, parallel to you, and perhaps within reach. Indeed, it is clear – even if by now this is the only thing that is – that if you clamber up on to the plank, you will sleep, that the plank is sleep itself. The principle of the operation is simplicity itself, even though you have every reason to believe that it will take you quite some time to accomplish: you would have to reduce the bed and the body to a single point, a marble, or perhaps, which amounts to the same thing, boil down the flaccidity of the body, concentrating it into a single spot, into one of the lumbar vertebrae, for example. But now the body no longer exhibits the fine unity that it possessed a moment ago: in fact it is spreading out in every direction. You try to draw in a toe towards the centre, or your thumb, or your thigh, but each time there is a rule you are forgetting, and this is that you must never lose sight of the hardness of the plank, that you should proceed with stealth, drawing in your body without it suspecting anything, without even knowing it yourself for certain, but it is too late, every time it is too late, and has been for a very long time, and, a strange consequence this, the bar of your eyebrows breaks in two, and in the middle, right between your eyes, as if this hinge had held everything else together, and as if all the force of the hinge were focused on this one spot, a precise and unmistakably conscious pain suddenly starts up, a pain which you recognise immediately as being nothing more extraordinary than a headache.

You ARE SITTING, naked from the waist up, wearing only pyjama bottoms, in your garret, on the narrow bench that serves as your bed, with a book, Raymond Aron's *Eighteen Lectures on Industrial Society*, resting on your knees, open at page one hundred and twelve.

At first it's just a sort of lassitude or tiredness, as if you suddenly became aware that for a long time, for several hours, you have been succumbing to an insidious, numbing discomfort, not exactly painful but nonetheless intolerable, succumbing to the sickly-sweet and stifling sensation of being without muscles or bones, of being a sack of potatoes surrounded by other sacks of potatoes.

The sun beats down on the zinc flashings on the roof. In front of you, at eye-level, on a whitewood shelf, there is a half-empty, rather grubby bowl of Nescafé, an almost empty bag of sugar, a cigarette burning down in a whitish mock opaline ashtray bearing an advertiser's logo.

Someone is moving around in the next room, coughing, dragging his feet, moving furniture, opening drawers. Drops of water are continually forming on the drinking-water tap on the landing. Noises drift up from Rue Saint-Honoré far below.

The bells of Saint-Roch chime two. You look up, you stop reading, but you had already stopped long ago. You put the open book down beside you on the bed. You reach out your hand, you stub out the cigarette which is smoking

137

in the ashtray, you finish your bowl of Nescafé: it is barely lukewarm, too sweet, on the bitter side.

You are soaked in sweat. You get up, you go over to the window and close it. You turn on the tap in the tiny washbasin, you pass a damp flannel over your forehead, the back of your neck, your shoulders. You curl up sideways on the narrow bench. You close your eyes. Your head is heavy, your legs numb.

Later, the day of your exam comes and you do not get up. It's not a premeditated action, or rather it's not an action at all, but an absence of action, an action you do not perform, actions that you avoid performing. You went to bed early, you slept peacefully, you had set the alarm clock, you heard it go off, you waited for it to go off, for several minutes at least, already woken by the heat, or by the light, or by the noise of the milkmen, the dustmen, or by the expectation itself.

Your alarm clock goes off, you do not stir, you remain in your bed, you close your eyes again. Other alarms start ringing in adjacent rooms. You hear the sounds of running water, doors closing, steps hurrying down the stairs. Rue Saint-Honoré begins to fill up with car noises, the screeching of tyres, the crunching of gears, toots on the horn. Blinds slam open, shopkeepers raise their iron shutters.

You do not move; you will not move. Someone else, your twin, a ghostly, conscientious double is perhaps performing in your stead, one by one, the actions you have eschewed: he gets up, washes, shaves, dresses, goes out. You let him bound down the stairs, run down the street, leap onto the moving bus, arrive on time, out of breath but triumphant, at the doors of the hall. Certificate of Advanced Study in General Sociology. First written paper.

You get up too late. Back there in the hall, studious or

bored heads are bowed pensively over their desks. The perhaps anxious glances of your friends all converge on your still-vacant seat. You will not set down on four, eight or twelve sheets of paper what you know, what you think, what you know you are supposed to think, about alienation, the workers, modernity and leisure, about white-collar workers or about automation, about our knowledge of others, about Marx as a rival of De Tocqueville, about Weber as an opponent of Lukacs. In any case, you wouldn't have said anything, because you don't know a great deal and you think nothing at all. Your seat remains vacant. You won't finish your degree, you won't begin a postgraduate thesis. You will study no more.

You make, as you do every day, a bowl of Nescafé; you add, as you do every day, a few drops of sweetened condensed milk. You don't wash, you hardly bother to dress. In a pink plastic bowl you place three pairs of socks to soak.

You don't go and wait for the candidates to come out of the examination hall to find out what questions were devised to test their perspicacity. Neither do you go and join your friends in the café, as custom would have demanded, like every other day, but more especially on this day of exceptional gravity. One of them, the following morning, will climb the six flights of stairs that lead to your room. You will recognise his footfall on the stairs, you will let him knock on your door, wait, knock again, a little louder, look on the lintel over the door for the key that you would often leave there if you were going out for a few minutes to fetch bread, coffee, cigarettes, a newspaper or the mail, you'll let him wait a while longer, knock gently, call your name quietly, hesitate, then stamp back down again.

He came back, later, and slipped a note under the door.

Then others came, the day after, the day after that, knocked, looked for the key, called your name, slipped notes under the door.

You read the notes and crumple them into a ball. The notes are to arrange meetings which you miss. You stay lying on your narrow bench, your hands crossed behind your neck, your knees up. You look at the ceiling and you discover the cracks, the bits flaking off, the stains, the uneven contours. You do not want to see anyone, or to talk, or think, or go out, or move.

It is on a day like this one, a little later, a little earlier, that you discover, without surprise, that something is wrong, that, without mincing words, you don't know how to live, that you will never know.

The sun beats down on the sheet metal of the roof. The heat in your garret is unbearable. You are sitting, wedged between the bed and the bookshelf, with a book open on your lap. You stopped reading it long ago. You are staring at a whitewood shelf, at a pink plastic bowl in which six socks are stagnating. The smoke from your cigarette, abandoned in the ashtray, rises, in an almost straight line, and then spreads out in a quivering blanket against the ceiling which is fissured by minute cracks.

Something was going to break, something has broken. You no longer feel – how to put it? – held up: it is as if some thing which, it seemed to you, it seems to you, fortified you until then, gave warmth to your heart, something like the feeling of your existence, of your importance almost, the impression of belonging to or of being in the world, is starting to slip away from you.

And yet you are not one of those people who spend their waking hours wondering if they exist, and why, where they came from, what they are, where they are going. You have never seriously agonised over the chicken and the egg. Metaphysical torments have not significantly ravaged your noble countenance. But nothing remains of that arrow-like trajectory, of that forward movement in which, for as long as you can remember, you have been led to recognise your life, that is to say its meaning, its truth, its tension: a past rich in fruitful experiences, lessons well learned, joyous childhood memories, sun-bathed country idylls, bracing sea breezes, a dense present, compact and taut, like a coiled spring, a productive, verdant, airy future. Your past, your present and your future merge into one: they are now just the heaviness of your limbs, your nagging migraine, your lassitude, the heat, the bitterness of the lukewarm Nescafé. And, if your life needed a setting, it would not be the majestic esplanade (by and large a spectacular trick of perspective) where the chubby-cheeked children of triumphant humanity fly past and frolic, but rather, irrespective of any effort you may make or any illusions you may still harbour, this converted cubbyhole that passes for your bedroom, this garret two metres ninety-two long by one metre seventy-three wide, that is to say, a little over five square metres, this attic from which you have not stirred for several hours, several days: you are sitting on a bed which is too short for you to be able to lie on it, full length, at night, and too narrow for you to be able to turn over on it, without extreme care. You are staring, almost fascinated now, at a pink plastic bowl which contains no fewer than six socks.

You stay in your room, without eating, without reading, almost without moving. You stare at the bowl, the shelf, your knees, your own gaze in the cracked mirror, the coffee-bowl, the light-switch. You listen to the sounds of the street, the dripping tap on the landing, the noises that your neighbour makes, clearing his throat, opening and closing drawers, coughing fits, the whistle of his kettle. you follow across the ceiling the sinuous lines of a thin crack, the futile meandering of a fly, the progress – which it is almost possible to plot – of the shadows.

This is your life. This is yours. You can establish an exact inventory of your meagre fortune, the precise balance sheet of your first quarter-century. You are twenty-five years old, you have twenty-nine teeth, three shirts and eight socks, a few books you no longer read, a few records you no longer play. You do not want to remember anything else, be it your family or your studies, your friends and lovers, or your holidays and plans. You travelled and you brought nothing back from your travels. Here you sit, and you want only to wait, just to wait until there is nothing left to wait for: for night to fall and the passing hours to chime, for the days to slip away and the memories to fade.

You do not see your friends again. You do not open your door. You do not go down to fetch your mail. You do not take back the books you borrowed from the Library of the Institute of Education. You do not write to your parents.

You only go out after nightfall, like the rats, the cats and the monsters. You drift around the streets, you slip into the grubby little cinemas on the Grands Boulevards. Sometimes you walk all night, sometimes you sleep all day.

You are a man of leisure, a sleepwalker, a mollusc. The definitions vary according to the hour of the day, or the day of the week, but the meaning remains clear enough: you do not really feel cut out for living, for doing, for making; you want only to go on, to go on waiting, and to forget.

Such an outlook on life is generally not much appreciated in modern times: all around you, all your life, you have seen the esteem in which action is held, and grand designs, and enthusiasm: man straining forward, man with his gaze fixed on the horizon, man looking straight ahead. A clear gaze, a purposeful chin, a confident swagger, stomach held in. Staying power, initiative, strokes of brilliance, success: all of these things map out the too transparent path of a too exemplary existence, constitute the sacrosanct images of the struggle for life. The white lies, the comforting illusions of all those who are running on the spot, sinking deeper into the mire, the lost illusions of the thousands left on society's scrap heap, those who arrived too late, those who put their suitcase down on the pavement and sat on it to wipe their brow. But you no longer need excuses, regrets, nostalgia. You reject nothing, you refuse nothing. You have ceased going forward, but that is because you weren't going forward anyway, you're not setting off again, you have arrived, you can see no reason to go any further: all it took, practically, on a day in May when it was too hot, was the untimely conjunction of a text of which you'd lost the thread, a bowl of Nescafé that suddenly tasted too bitter, and a pink plastic bowl filled with blackish water in which six socks were floating, this was all it took for something to snap, to turn bad, to come undone, and for the truth to appear in the bright light of day – but the light of day is never bright in the garret on Rue Saint-Honoré – this disappointing truth, as sad and ridiculous as a dunce's cap, as heavy as a Latin dictionary: you have no desire to carry on, no desire to defend yourself, no desire to attack.

Your friends got tired of knocking on your door. Now, you rarely ever frequent the streets where you might run into them. You avoid the questions and the eyes of strangers whom chance occasionally places in your path, you refuse the beer or the coffee they offer you. Only the night and your room protect you: the narrow bed where you lie stretched out, the ceiling that you discover anew at every moment; the night in which, alone amidst the crowds on the Grands Boulevards, you occasionally feel almost happy with the noise and the lights, the bustle and the forgetting. You have no need to speak, to desire. You follow the tide as it ebbs and flows, from Place de la République to Place de la Madeleine, from Place de la Madeleine to Place de la République.

You are not in the habit of making diagnoses, and you don't want to start now. What is worrying you, what is disturbing you, what is frightening you, but which now and then gives you a thrill, is not the suddenness of your metamorphosis, but precisely the opposite: the vague and heavy feeling that it isn't a metamorphosis at all, that nothing has changed, that you've always been like this, even though you only now realize it fully: that thing, in the cracked mirror, is not your new face, it is just that the masks have slipped, the heat in your room has melted them, your torpor has soaked them off. The masks of unswerving conviction, of the straight and narrow. Did you never have an inkling, not once in twenty-five years, of that which, today, has already become inexorable? Did you never see any cracks in what, for you, takes the place of a history? Times when nothing was happening, times when you were simply ticking over in neutral. The fleeting and poignant desire to hear no more, to see no more, to remain silent and motionless. Crazy dreams of solitude. An amnesiac wandering through the Land of the Blind: wide, empty streets, cold lights, faces without mouths that you would look at without seeing. They would never get to you.

It is as if, beneath the surface of your calm and reassuring history (the good little boy, the model pupil, the dependable pal), as if, running beneath the obvious, too obvious, signs of growth and maturity – scribbled graffiti on toilet doors, certificates, long trousers, the first cigarette, the sting of the first shave, alcohol, the key left under the mat for your Saturday night outings, losing your virginity, the baptism of air, the baptism of fire – as if another thread had always been running, ever present but always held at bay, and which is now weaving the familiar fabric of your rediscovered existence, the bare backdrop of your abandoned life, memories which suddenly resurface, veiled images of this revealed truth, of this resignation so long deferred, of this appeal for calm – hazy and lifeless images, over-exposed snapshots, almost white, almost dead, almost already fossilised: a street in a sleepy provincial town, closed shutters, dull shadows, the buzzing of flies in an army post, a lounge draped in grey dustsheets, particles suspended in a ray of sunlight, bare countryside, cemeteries on a Sunday, outings in a car.

Man sitting on a narrow bed, one Thursday afternoon, a book open on his knees, eyes vacant.

You are just a murky shadow, a hard kernel of indifference, a neutral gaze avoiding the gaze of others. Speechless lips, dead eyes. Henceforth you will be able to glimpse in the puddles, in the shop windows, in the gleaming bodywork of cars, the fleeting reflections of your decelerating life.

Absent-mindedly, you let your hand slip along the white-wood shelf. Water drips from the tap on the landing. Your neighbour is sleeping. The faint chugging of a stationary diesel taxi emphasises rather than breaks the silence of the street. Your memory is slowly penetrated by oblivion. Nothing has happened. Nothing will ever happen. The cracks in the ceiling trace an implausible labyrinth.

There were those empty days, the heat in your room, like a cauldron, like a furnace, and the six socks, indolent sharks, sleeping whales, in the pink plastic bowl. That alarm clock that did not ring, that does not ring, that will not ring to wake you up. You put down the open book beside you on the bed, you stretch out. The sluggish, dull, throb of torpor. You let yourself slip. You drop into sleep.

FIRST THERE ARE SOME FAMILIAR or obsessive images; playing cards spread out before you that you pick up and put down endlessly, without ever succeeding in ordering them in the way you would like, and the unpleasant impression of needing to finish, to succeed in this ordering, as if the revelation of some essential truth depended on it, but it is always the same card that you pick up, lay down and place in order, then pick up, lay down and place in order all over again; crowds walking up and down, coming and going; walls that surround you and in which you search for a concealed exit, the hidden button that will make the walls swing back or the ceiling lift off; forms which take shape then slip away, return then disappear, get closer then fade, flames or dancing women, shadow-play.

Later, memories that no longer quite manage to make their way through, proofs that no longer prove anything, except, perhaps, that an observatory in Aberdeen, or Inverness, has indeed succeeded in picking up signals from distant stars: was it the Andromeda Nebula, or the Goll and Burdach Constellation? Or the Corpora quadrigemina? The immediate, obvious solution to a problem that has always bothered you: the knight is never master in hearts unless the falsetto has been discarded. Disjointed words bearing a tangled meaning turn in a circle around you. What man imprisoned in a house of cards? What thread? What Law?

You must be precise, logical. Proceed methodically. There comes a point when you must, at all costs, be able to stop, reflect, really weigh up the situation. If there is a lake in the middle of your head, a possibility that is not only plausible, but quite normal, even though it may not be asserted without qualification, then it will take you a certain amount of time to reach it. There is no path, there never is a path, and, near the lakeside, you'll have to be careful of the tall grass which is always dangerous at this time of year. There won't be a rowing boat either, naturally, there hardly ever is, but you can swim across.

Subsequently, there obviously never was a lake. You remember quite distinctly that there never has been a lake. However, for quite some time now, sleep has been right in front of you, closer than it has ever been. It has its usual shape: the ball, or rather the bubble, the big, enormous bubble, transparent, of course, but not made of glass, it's more like soap in fact, but a very hard soap, not at all fatty, and only very slightly crumbly, or else, perhaps, like a very thin, very taut membrane. All of its characteristics are there. You don't even have to look for them in order to know this, it simply goes without saying, all you need do is enumerate them: at the top the bubble is turning pink, the bit in front of you is desquamating, at the side it is trying feebly to breathe; the rest belongs to the pillow around which you are wrapped, and to which you are securely lashed, thanks to the pressure that you exert without undue effort on the loop formed by the thumb and index finger of your right hand.

Now it's getting a lot more difficult. For one thing, it's becoming obvious that the bubble has cheated; it is not in the least bit spherical, but more fish-shaped, like a spindle-fish; what is more, its translucidity is of an altogether mediocre quality, scarcely superior to that of the pillow; finally, and above all, it is certainly not in the process of turning pink at the top. The only thing that was, perhaps, for certain, is this desquamation which has very quickly accelerated, and the breathing that was weak but which is now deep. But the most troublesome aspect is the temperature of the whole which has risen rapidly and will shortly reach a critical threshold – an eventuality which is doubtless heralded by these increasingly numerous desquamations.

The situation is awkward. You were wrong to pay attention to these details that were not even true; quite clearly, they were just traps, and now you are well and truly a prisoner inside the pillow where it is so hot and dark that you are wondering, not without a degree of anxiety, how you are going to go about extricating yourself. Fortunately, it's not the first time that you've found yourself in this situation; you know that you have only to find an undulation in the landscape, on the horizon, or a faint glimmer in the darkness, a lake, or a cool place you can slip into; and it so happens that you find yourself extraordinarily well-disposed to the idea of letting yourself slip. But search as you may, there is nothing before you, no horizon, no faint glimmer, no lake, nothing, just the dark, thick, stifling pillow. This doesn't surprise you, you were half expecting it. You notice that you weren't really shut in, that, all this time, sleep, real sleep, was behind you, not in front of you, behind you and so recognisable with its long grey beaches, its frosty horizon, its black sky shot through with white or grey streaks. You notice it all of a sudden, you recognise it immediately, but it is too late to reach it, as it always is; another time perhaps. There is something else you know as well, or rather something that you should have been able to foresee: you should never turn round, or at any rate not so quickly, or everything breaks, higgledy-piggledy, your pillow falls and takes your cheek with it, your fore-arm, your thumb and your feet topple over on top of each other: the tiny grey window takes its place again, close by, once more the dungeon with sloping walls takes shape, and locks shut. You are sitting on your bed.

LATER YOU LEAVE PARIS; you do not set off at random, you go to your parents' house in the countryside near Auxerre. It's a rather dead little village, where your parents live in retirement. You spent a few years there as a child, and a few vacations. The ruins of a castle stand atop a hill at the foot of which the village has grown up. Apparently, a beatific hermit once lived in a nearby cave which is now open to visitors. In the square, near the church, there is a tree reputed to be several hundred years old.

You stay there for several months. At mealtimes you listen to the news and the quiz programmes on the radio. In the evenings you play *belote* with your father, who wins. You go to bed very early, before your parents, at nine o'clock. Sometimes you read all through the night. You have rediscovered in your room, in the loft, hidden away in linen cupboards, the books you read when you were fifteen, Alexandre Dumas, Jules Verne, Jack London, and the piles of detective novels that you brought with you on each of your previous visits. You re-read them carefully, without skipping a line, as if you had completely forgotten them, as if you had never really read them.

You hardly say a word to your parents, you scarcely see them outside of meal-times. In the morning you lounge around in bed. You can hear them moving about the house, going up- and downstairs, coughing, opening drawers. Your father is sawing wood. A grocery van sounds its horn near the gate. A dog barks, birds sing, the church bells ring. Lying in your high bed with the feather quilt pulled right up to your chin, you study the ceiling joists, a tiny spider with a grey, almost white abdomen, is spinning its web in the corner of a beam.

You sit down at the kitchen table with its waxed table-cloth. Your mother pours you a bowl of white coffee, and pushes the bread, the jam and the butter towards you. You eat in silence. She talks to you about her kidney problems, your father, the neighbours, the village. Madame Thevenon has sold her farm in return for an annuity. The Moreaus' dog has died. Work on the new motorway has already begun.

You go down into the village to run a few errands for your mother, to buy tobacco for your father and cigarettes for yourself. The farmers have deserted what was once a sizeable village. Trains used to stop here, there was a solicitor, a market; only two agricultural holdings remain. Nowadays the village is inhabited by retired people and city folk who come for the weekend and a month each summer, doubling or tripling the winter population.

You walk past the restored houses: shutters repainted in apple-green, adorned with wrought-iron *fleurs-de-lys*, antique dealers' carriage-lamps, ornamental gardens, grottoes where no deities reside, a weekenders' paradise. Lawyers, grocers and civil servants trim the hedges, rake the gravel paths, fuss over their borders and feed the goldfish. The square is dotted with clusters of mopeds and scooters belonging to the youngsters. The *café-tabac* is full of people.

Every afternoon you go for a walk. You stick to the road at first, and then, beyond a disused quarry, you plunge into the forest. You pick up a branch that you roughly strip of its twigs. You walk beside fields of ripe wheat. You lop the heads off weeds with great clumsy swipes of your stick. You do not know the names of the trees, nor of the flowers, the plants, the clouds. You sit down on top of a hill from where you can survey the whole village: your parents' house, somewhat on the outskirts, with its three roofs of different colours, the castle on about the same level as your eyes, the viaduct that used to carry the railway line, the laundry, the post office. On the white road far below, a huge lorry moves away like a galleon leaving port. A solitary peasant, in the middle of his field, guides a plough pulled by a dappled horse.

Bird-song rings out: chirps, roulades, raucous cries. The great trees tremble. Nature is there and it beckons you lovingly. You chew on blades of grass that you quickly spit out: you are not really inspired by the landscape, or moved by the tranquillity of the fields, you are neither irritated nor soothed by the silence of the countryside. You are only occasionally fascinated by an insect, a stone, a fallen leaf, a tree: sometimes you spend hours contemplating a tree, describing it, dissecting it: the roots, the trunk, the branches, the leaves, every leaf, every rib of every leaf, every branch again, and the unending play of the indifferent shapes that your eager gaze solicits or conjures up: a face, a town, a maze or a path, coats of arms and cavalcades. As your perception gets sharper, more patient and more versatile, the tree shatters and then reforms, a thousand shades of green, a thousand leaves, identical and yet all different. You think that you could spend your whole life in front of a tree, never exhausting it and never understanding it, because there is nothing for you to understand, just something to look at: when all is said and done, all you can say about this tree is that it is a tree; all this tree can say to you is that it is a tree, a root, then a trunk, then branches, then leaves. You can't expect to extract any other truth from it. The tree has no moral to offer you, no message to impart.

Its strength, its majesty, its life – if you still hope to draw some meaning, some courage, from these outworn metaphors – are only ever images, neat illustrations, as useless as the tranquillity of the fields, as the still waters which, reputedly, run deep, or the courage of the little paths that don't climb very high but do so all alone, or the smiling hillsides upon which bunches of grapes ripen in the sun.

And that is why the tree fascinates you, or astounds you, or calms you: because of the unsuspected and unimpeachable obviousness of the bark, the branches and the leaves. That is why, perhaps, you never go walking with a dog, because the dog looks at you, pleads with you, speaks to you. Its eyes brimming with tears of gratitude, its servile expression, its canine frolicking, constantly force you to confer on it the ignoble status of pet. You cannot remain neutral in the company of a dog any more than in the company of a man. But you will never hold a conversation with a tree. You cannot live in the company of a dog, because the dog is constantly calling upon you to make it live, to feed it, to stroke it, to be a man for it, to be its master, to be the god roaring the name – dog – that will make it instantly grovel on the ground. But the tree asks nothing of you. You can be the God of the dogs, God of the cats, God of the poor, all you need is a leash, a little tenderness, a little money, but you will never be master of the tree. All you can ever wish for is to become a tree in your turn.

It is not that you hate men, why would you hate them? Why would you hate yourself? If only membership of the human race were not accompanied by this insufferable din, if only these few pathetic steps taken into the animal kingdom did not have to be bought at the cost of this perpetual, nauseous dyspepsia of words, projects, great departures! But it is too high a price to pay for opposable thumbs, an erect stature, the incomplete rotation of the head on the shoulders: this cauldron, this furnace, this grill which is life, these thousands of summonses, incitements, warnings, thrills, depressions, this enveloping atmosphere of obligations, this eternal machine for producing, crushing, swallowing up, overcoming obstacles, starting afresh and without respite, this insidious terror which seeks to control every day, every hour of your meagre existence!

You have hardly started living, and yet all is said, all is done. You are only twenty-five, but your path is already mapped out for you. The roles are prepared, and the labels: from the potty of your infancy to the bath-chair of your old age, all the seats are ready and waiting their turn. Your adventures have been so thoroughly described that the most violent revolt would not make anyone turn a hair. Step into the street and knock people's hats off, smear your head with filth, go bare-foot, publish manifestos, shoot at some passing usurper or other, but it won't make any difference: in the dormitory of the asylum your bed is already made up, your place is already laid at the table of the *poètes maudits*; Rimbaud's drunken boat, what a paltry wonder: Abyssinia is a fairground attraction, a package trip. Everything is arranged, everything is prepared in the minutest detail: the surges of emotion, the frosty irony, the heartbreak, the fullness, the exoticism, the great adventure, the despair. You won't sell your soul to the devil, you won't go clad in sandals to throw yourself into the crater of Mount Etna, you won't destroy the seventh wonder of the world. Everything is ready for your death: the bullet that will end your days was cast long ago, the weeping women who will follow your casket have already been appointed.

Why climb to the peak of the highest hills when you would only have to come back down again, and, when you are down, how would you avoid spending the rest of your life telling the story of how you got up there? Why should you keep up the pretence of living? Why should you carry on? Don't you already know everything that will happen to you? Haven't you already been all that you were meant to be: the worthy son of your mother and father, the brave little boy scout, the good pupil who could have done better, the childhood friend, the distant cousin, the handsome soldier, the impoverished young man? Just a little more effort, not even a little more effort, just a few more years, and you will be the middle manager, the esteemed colleague. Good husband, good father, good citizen. War veteran. One by one, you will climb, like a frog, the rungs on the ladder of success. You'll be able to choose, from an extensive and varied range, the personality that best befits your aspirations, it will be carefully tailored to measure: will you be decorated? cultured? an epicure? a physician of body and soul? an animal lover? will you devote your spare time to massacring, on an out-of-tune piano, innocent sonatas that never did you any harm? Or will you smoke a pipe in your rocking chair, telling yourself that, all in all, life's been good to you?

No. You prefer to be the missing piece of the puzzle. You're getting out while the going's good. You're not stacking any odds in your favour or putting any eggs in any baskets. You're putting the cart before the horse, you're throwing the helve after the hatchet, you're counting your chickens before they're hatched and eating the calf in the belly of the cow, you're drinking your liquid assets, taking French leave, you are leaving and you are not looking back.

You won't listen to any more sound advice. You won't ask for any remedies. You will go your own way, you will look to the trees, the water, the stones, the sky, your face, the clouds, the ceiling, the void.

You remain near the tree. You don't even ask the rush of the wind in the leaves to become your oracle.

The rain comes. You stay indoors, you hardly set foot outside your room. You read aloud, all day long, following the lines of text with your finger, like a child or an old man, until the words lose their meaning, until the simplest phrase becomes cock-eyed and chaotic. Evening comes. You don't switch on the light and you remain motionless, sitting at the little table by the window with the book in your hands but no longer reading, listening distractedly to the sounds of the house, the creaking of the beams and the floorboards, your father's coughing, the cast-iron hotplates being fitted onto the wood-fired stove, the noise of the rain in the zinc valleys, a car passing, far away, the seven o'clock bus sounding its horn as it rounds the turning near the hill.

The summer visitors have all departed. The holiday homes are closed up. When you go into the village, the occasional dog barks at you as you walk past. Tattered posters, on the church square, by the town hall, the post-office, the laundry, are still advertising auction sales, dances, village fêtes held long ago.

You still go for the odd walk. You tread the same old paths. You cross ploughed fields which leave thick layers of clay sticking to the soles of your boots. You get bogged down in the ruts in the pathways. The sky is grey. The views are obscured by blankets of mist. Smoke rises from a few chimneys. You are cold despite your lined pea-jacket, your boots, your gloves; you clumsily attempt to light a cigarette.

You venture further afield, towards other villages, across the fields and through the woods. You sit at the long wooden table of a grocery store-cum-bar where you are the only customer. You are served a cup of Bovril or an insipid coffee. Dozens of flies blacken the fly-paper that still hangs in a spiral from the enamelled lampshade. An uninterested cat is warming itself by the cast-iron stove. You study the shelves of tins, the packs of washing powder, the aprons, the exercise-books, the already out-of-date newspapers, the candy-pink postcards on which chubby soldiers give voice to the elevated sentiments inspired in them by some blonde sweetheart, the bus timetables, the racing results, the results of the Sunday football matches.

Flights of birds drift past high overhead. On the Yonne canal, a long barge with a metallic blue hull slips by, pulled by two big greys. You return on foot along the main road, in the darkness, cars roar past you in both directions, you are dazzled by their headlamps which, from the hollows of the hills, seem momentarily to be trying to light up the skies before bearing down on you.

YOU RETURN TO PARIS and the same room, the same silence. The dripping tap, the crowds, the streets, the bridges; the ceiling, the pink plastic bowl; the narrow bed. The cracked mirror in which the features that make up your face are reflected.

Your room is the centre of the world. This lair, this cupboard-like garret which never loses your smell, with its bed into which you slip alone, its shelf, its linoleum, its ceiling whose cracks and flakes, stains and contours you have counted a thousand times, the washbasin that is so tiny it resembles a piece of doll's-house furniture, the bowl, the window, the wallpaper of which you know every flower, every stem, every interlacement, details which – as you alone are able to state with absolute certainty – are never quite identical to each other, despite the virtual infallibility of printing methods; these newspapers that you read and re-read, that you will read and re-read again; this cracked mirror that has only ever reflected your face fragmented into three uneven, slightly overlapping, surface portions that habit almost allows you to ignore, forgetting the ghostly image of an eye in the middle of your forehead, or the split nose, or the perpetually twisted mouth, and retaining only a Y-shaped stripe, like the almost forgotten, partially erased mark of some old wound, a slash from a sabre or the lash of a whip; the shelved books, the ribbed radiator, the portable record-player sheathed in dark red pegamoid: thus begins and ends your kingdom, perfectly encircled by the hosts of ever-present noises – some friendly, some hostile – which are now all that keep you attached to the world: the dripping tap on the landing, the noises from your neighbour's room, his throat-clearing, the drawers which he opens and closes, his coughing fits, the whistling of his kettle, the noises of Rue Saint-Honoré, the incessant rumble of the city. From far away, the siren of a fire engine seems to be heading straight for you, then moving away, then drawing closer again. At the junction of Rue Saint-Honoré and Rue des Pyramides the measured succession of car noises, braking, stopping, pulling away, accelerating, imparts a rhythm to time almost as surely as the tirelessly dripping tap or the bells of Saint-Roch.

Your alarm clock has been showing five-fifteen for a long time now. It stopped, probably when you were out, and you haven't bothered to wind it up again. Time no longer penetrates into the silence of your room, it is all around, a permanent medium, even more present and obsessive than the hands of a clock that you could choose not to look at, and yet slightly warped, out of true, somehow suspect: time passes, but you never know what time it is, the chimes of Saint-Roch do not distinguish the quarter-hours from the halves, or the three-quarters, the traffic-lights at the junction of Rue Saint-Honoré and Rue des Pyramides do not change every minute, the tap does not drip every second. It is ten o'clock, or perhaps eleven, for how can you be sure that you heard correctly, it's late, it's early, the sun rises, night falls, the sounds never quite cease altogether, time never stops completely, even if it is now reduced to the merely imperceptible: a hairline crack in the wall of silence, the forgotten murmur of the drip-feed, almost indistinguishable from the beats of your heart.

★

Your room is the most beautiful of desert islands, and Paris is a desert that no-one has ever traversed. All you really need is your sleep, silence around you, your own silence, stillness. All you need is for days to begin and end, for time to pass, for your mouth to be shut, for the muscles in your nape, your jaws and your chin to slacken, for the rising and falling of your rib-cage, the beating of your heart to be the only evidence of your continuing and patient existence.

To want nothing. Just to wait, until there is nothing left to wait for. Just to wander, and to sleep. To let yourself be carried along by the crowds, and the streets. To follow the gutters, the fences, the water's edge. To walk the length of the embankments, to hug the walls. To waste your time. To have no projects, to feel no impatience. To be without desire, or resentment, or revolt.

In the course of time your life will be there in front of you: a life without motion, without crisis and without disorder, a life with no rough edges and no imbalance. Minute by minute, hour after hour, day after day, season after season, something is going to start that will be without end: your vegetal existence, your cancelled life.

NOW YOU LEARN HOW TO LAST. At times, you are the master of time itself, the master of the world, a watchful little spider at the hub of your web, reigning over Paris: you command the North by Avenue de l'Opéra, the South by the Louvre colonnade, the East and West by Rue Saint-Honoré.

At times, you attempt to solve the puzzle of a face which emerges, perhaps, from the complex play of shadows and blisters in a portion of the ceiling: eyes and nose, nose and mouth, a forehead uninterrupted by any hairline, or else it is the precise outline of the helix of an ear, the beginings of a shoulder and a neck.

There are a thousand ways to kill time and no two are the same, but each is as good as the next, a thousand ways of waiting for nothing, a thousand games that you can invent and then drop straightaway.

You have everything still to learn, everything that cannot be learnt: solitude, indifference, patience, silence. You must become unused to everything: you must lose the habit of going to meet those with whom you rubbed shoulders for so long, of taking your meals and your cups of coffee every day at the place that others have kept, sometimes defended, for you, of languishing in the insipid complicity of friendships that linger on but just won't die, in the opportunist and cowardly rancour of affairs that are coming apart at the seams.

You are alone, and because you are alone you must never look to see what time it is, never count the minutes. You must never again eagerly tear open your mail, never again be disappointed when all you find is advertising bumph inviting you to acquire, for the modest sum of seventy-seven francs, a cake set engraved with your monogram, or the treasures of Western art.

You must forget hope, enterprise, success, perseverance.

You are letting yourself go, and it comes almost easily to you. You avoid the paths which you followed for too long. You allow passing time to erase the memory of the faces, the telephone numbers and the addresses, the smiles and the voices.

You forget that you learnt how to forget, that, one day, you forced yourself to forget. Now you wander up and down Boulevard Saint-Michel without recognising anything, not seeing the shop windows, not seen by the streams of students who pass you by. You no longer enter the cafés, checking all the tables with a worried expression on your face, going into the back rooms in search of you no longer know whom. You no longer look for anyone in the queues which form every two hours outside the seven cinemas in Rue Champollion. No longer do you wander like a lost soul in the great courtyard of the Sorbonne, or pace up and down the long corridors waiting for the lecture-rooms to empty, or go off to solicit greetings, smiles or signs of recognition in the library.

You are alone. You learn to walk like a man alone, to stroll, to dawdle, to see without looking, to look without seeing. You learn the art of transparency, immobility, inexistence. You learn how to be a shadow and how to look at men as if they were stones. You learn how to remain seated, or supine, or erect. You learn how to chew every mouthful of food, how to rediscover the same inert taste in every piece of food you raise to your mouth. You learn how to look at paintings in art galleries as if they were bits of wall or ceiling, and how to look at the walls and ceiling as if they were paintings whose tens and thousands of paths you follow untiringly, endlessly retracing your steps, as if they were merciless labyrinths, or a text that no-one will ever decipher, or decaying faces.

You plunge into Ile Saint-Louis, you take Rue Vaugirard and head towards Péreire, towards Château-Landon. You walk slowly, and return the way you came, sticking close to the shop fronts: the window-displays of hardware stores, electrical shops, haberdashers', second-hand furniture dealers. You go and sit on the parapet of Pont Louis-Philippe and you watch an eddy forming and disintegrating under the arches, the funnel-shaped depression perpetually deepening and then filling up, in front of the cutwaters. Further out, horse-drawn and motorised barges pass by, eventually shattering the play of water against the piers. Motionless anglers sit, the length of the embankment, their eyes following the inexorable drift of their floats.

Sitting outside a café with a glass of beer or a coffee in front of you, you watch the street. Cars, taxis, vans, buses, motorbikes and mopeds pass by in compact clusters, separated by occasional brief lulls: distant echoes of the traffic lights that regulate the flow of vehicles. On the pavements, continuous but much more fluid, the double bands of pedestrians stream past. Two men carrying identical imitation leather document cases pass by each other, with the same weary gait; a mother and daughter, children, old ladies carrying heavy shopping bags, a soldier, a man weighed down by two heavy suitcases, and still others, with packages, newspapers, pipes, umbrellas, dogs, paunches, hats, prams, uniforms, some of them almost running, others dragging their feet, stopping in front of the shop windows, greeting each other, bidding farewell, overtaking or simply passing each other by, old and young, men and women, happy and unhappy. Groups, continually disbanding and reforming, pile up at the bus-stops. A sandwich-man hands out advertising leaflets. A woman tries in vain to flag down a passing taxi. The siren of a fire-engine or a police car comes towards you, growing louder.

A breakdown lorry roars past on its way to some unknown emergency. You know nothing of the laws which preside over the meeting of all these people, these people who do not know each other and whom you do not know, in this street that you are visiting for the first time in your life and where you have no business to attend to, except to watch the crowds coming and going, surging forward, stopping. All these feet on the pavements, all these wheels on the road, what are they all doing here? Where are they all going? What calls them together? Why do they return? What kind of force, or mystery, makes them place first the right foot, then the left, on the pavement, with a coordination that could scarcely be more efficient? Thousands of futile actions come together in the same instant in the too-narrow field of your almost neutral vision. They extend their right hands simultaneously and give a crushing hand-shake, their mouths emit apparently meaningful messages, their speech is punctuated by expressive mimes: their hands flutter, they contort their cheeks, noses, eyebrows, lips; they get out their diaries, pass each other by, greet, berate, congratulate, jostle each other; they head towards you without seeing you, and yet you are just a few inches away, sitting on the terrace of a café, and you do not take your eyes off them.

You drift around. You imagine a classification of streets, *quartiers*, apartment blocks: the crazy *quartiers*, the dead *quartiers*, the market streets, the dormitory streets, the cemetery streets, the peeling façades, the worn façades, the rusty façades, the concealed façades.

You walk round the fenced gardens, overtaken by children clattering an iron or wooden ruler against the palings as they run past. You sit down on the benches with green slats and cast-iron lion-paw ferrules. Disabled, ageing park-keepers pass the time of day with nannies of a different generation. With the tip of your shoes you trace circles on the sparsely sandy ground, or squares, or an eye, or your initials.

You discover streets where cars never pass, in which it appears that practically nobody lives, streets with a single ghost shop, a ladies' fashion shop, its window hung with net curtains and containing a display that seems to have been there for ever: the same pale mannequin faded by the sun, the same trays of dress-buttons, the same fashion plates which, nevertheless, bear this year's date; or a mattress maker displaying his springs, his olive-wood bed-legs in the shape of a ball or a spindle, his various grades of horse-hair and ticking, or perhaps a cobbler in his little recess which serves as a workshop, and whose door consists simply of curtains made from multicoloured plastic beads threaded on lengths of nylon line.

You discover the arcades: Choiseul, Panoramas, Jouffroy, Verdeau. You discover their stores selling scale models, pipes, paste jewellery, stamps, the shoe-shine boys and hot-dog stands. You read, one after the other, the faded cards displayed in a typesetter's window: Doctor Raphaël Crubellier, Stomatologist, Graduate of the Faculty of Medicine of Paris, by appointment only, 'Marcel-Emile Burnachs Ltd. *Tout pour le Tapis*', Monsieur and Madame Serge Valène, 11, Rue Lagarde, 214 07 35; Collège Geoffroy

Saint-Hilaire Old Boys' Association Annual Dinner, Menu: *Les Délices de la mer sur le lit des glaciers, le Bloc du Périgord aux perles noires, la Belle argentée du lac.*

In the Luxembourg Gardens you watch the pensioners playing bridge, *belote* or *tarot*. On a bench close by an old man stares into space for hours on end; he is mummified, perfectly still, with his heels together and his chin leaning on the knob of the walking-stick that he grips tightly with both hands. You marvel at him. You try to discover his secret, his weakness. But he appears to have no weak point. He must be as deaf as a post, half-blind and verging on the paralytic. But he doesn't even dribble, or move his lips, he hardly even blinks. The sun describes an arc about him: perhaps his vigilance consists solely in following his shadow; he must have markers placed long in advance; his madness, if he is mad, consists in believing that he is a sundial. He resembles a statue, but he has an advantage over statues in that he is capable of getting up and walking, if he so desires. He also resembles a human being, despite his head which is more birdlike than human, and his trousers hitched right up to his sternum, and his primary school teacher's butterfly-bow, but he has this ability, denied to other men, of being able to remain as motionless as a statue, for hours on end, with no apparent effort. You would like to be able to do this yourself, but – and this is probably one of the effects of your being so young and inexperienced in the art of being old – you get restless too quickly: you let your eyes wander in spite of yourself, your foot starts scuffing the sand, you are continually crossing and uncrossing your fingers.

Still you keep walking, wherever your feet take you. You get lost, you go round in circles. Sometimes you set yourself derisory goals: Daumesnil, Clignancourt,

Boulevard Gouvion Saint-Cyr or the Postal Museum. You wander into bookshops and leaf through a few books without reading them. You go to art galleries, doing a complete round, stopping conscientiously in front of every painting, leaning your head to the right, squinting, moving up close so as to be able to read the title, or the date, or the artist's name, stepping back to get a better view. On your way out, you sign the book with large illegible initials accompanied by a false address.

You sit at a table at the back of a café and read *Le Monde*, line by line, systematically. It is an excellent exercise. You read the headlines on the front page, the foreign reports, the short items on the back page, the classifed advertisements: situations vacant, employment wanted, sales represen-tation, business opportunities, properties and estates, land, flats (for sale), flats (new developments), flats (wanted), offices to let, commercial property, businesses for sale, investments, partnerships, tuition, annuities, cars, lock-up garages, pets, second-hand, receptions, births, engage-ments, marriages, obituaries, acknowledgements, auctions at the Drouot Sales Room, lectures and meetings, univer-sity *vivas*; the crossword which you practically solve in your head (cry, we hear, in one's cups: wine; a demonstra-tive in the sentence: these; you won't find this chopper in your knife-drawer!: egg-beater; a number boil wildly in your tank: Mobil; distraught armadillo loses fifty-love to the commander: admiral); the weather forecast; radio and television, theatre and cinema programmes, the stock mar-ket; the pages covering: travel, society, food, the economy, books, sport, science, the universities, theatre, medicine, women, the regions, education, religion, aeronautics, legal affairs, the unions, world affairs, foreign news, French politics, home affairs, news in brief, the in-depth specials stretching over three or four issues, supplements devoted to a country or a region or a particular product, the display advertisements.

Five hundred, a thousand pieces of information have passed in front of those eyes of yours, eyes so scrupulous and attentive that they even noticed the number of copies printed, and checked, once again, that this edition was produced by workers who are members of, and regulated by, the BVP and the OJD. But your memory has carefully avoided retaining any of this. You read with an equal lack of interest that Pont-à-Mousson was weak and that steel was losing ground whilst the New York market remained steady, that one may have complete confidence in the experience of the oldest credit bank in France and its network of specialists, that the damage caused in Florida by typhoon Barbara would cost three billion dollars to repair, that Jean-Paul and Lucas are proud to announce the arrival of their little sister Lucie: reading *Le Monde* is simply a way of wasting, or gaining, an hour or two, of measuring once again the extent of your indifference. All hierarchies and preferences must crumble and collapse. You are still capable of being amazed by the way in which the combination, according to a few ultimately very simple rules, of thirty or so typographic signs is able to generate, every day, these thousands of messages. But why should you eagerly devour them, why should you bother deciphering them? All that matters to you is that time should pass and that nothing should get through to you: your eyes follow the lines, deliberately, one after the other.

Indifference to the world is neither ignorance nor hostility. You do not propose to rediscover the robust joys of illiteracy, but rather, in reading, not to grant a privileged status to any one thing you read. You do not propose to go naked, but to be clad, without this implying either elegance or neglect; you do not propose to let yourself starve to death, but simply to feed yourself. It is not exactly that you seek to accomplish these actions in total innocence, for innocence is such a loaded term: but merely, simply (if this 'simply' can still mean anything) to relegate these actions to some neutral, self-contained territory, a space cleansed of all value-judgements, but not, especially not, a functional space: the functional is the worst, the most insidious, the most compromising of all values. No, let this space be self-evident, factual, irreducible. Let there be nothing else to say except: you read, you are clothed, you eat, you sleep, you walk, let these be actions or gestures, but not proofs, not some kind of symbolic currency: your dress, your food, your reading matter will not speak in your stead, you have had enough of trying to outsmart them. Never again will you entrust to them the exhausting, impossible, mortal burden of representing you.

From now on, when you eat standing up at the counter of La Petite Source or La Bière or Roger La Frite, it is rather like what psychophysiologists call "nutritional intake": you ingest, once or twice a day, rarely more, a fairly precisely calculable compound of proteins and glucosides, in the form of a piece of grilled beef, strips of potato quick-fried in boiling oil, and a glass of red wine. In other words it's a steak, sometimes called a minute steak, or even a rump steak, but it is definitely not a tournedos, and chips that no-one would dignify with the name French fries, and a glass of red wine of uncertain, not to say dubious, origin, and entirely unguaranteed quality. But your stomach can no longer tell the difference, if it ever could, and neither can your palate. Language has proved more resistant: it took a while for your meat to stop being thin, tough, stringy, for your chips to stop being greasy and soft, and the wine sticky or vinegary. It took a while for these eminently pejorative adjectives, which at first evoke the sad fare of the poorhouse, food for tramps, soup-kitchens, suburban fun-fairs, gradually to lose their substance, and for the sadness, the misery, the poverty, the need, the shame that had become inexorably attached to them – this fat-become-chip, this hardness-become-meat, this bitterness-become-wine – to stop hitting you, to stop leaving their mark on you. Similarly, it took a while for you to stop being convinced by the signs which are their exact opposite, the noble signs of abundance, feasting and merry-making: the bloody, succulent thickness of the 'sides' of Charolais or the 'slabs' of beef, of the finest fillet or porterhouse steaks, the golden crispness of straw potatoes, or match-stick potatoes, or soufflé potatoes, or *gratin dauphinois*, the bouquet of the fine wine in its wicker basket. Never again will your plate play host to any hallowed energy, and no divine nectar will sparkle in your glass. No exclamation marks punctuate your meals. You eat meat and chips and you drink wine. The immeasurable distance between a lavish Côte de boeuf de La Villette and the full-course menu that you order every day, as soon as you enter, from the counter at La Petite Source, no longer has any power over you.

COME RAIN OR SHINE, come fair weather or foul, whether the wind gusts or nary a leaf stirs on the trees, still you keep walking; whether dawn switches out the streetlamps or dusk turns them on again, whether you are swamped by the crowds or alone in a deserted square, still you keep walking, drifting.

You devise complicated itineraries, bristling with rules which oblige you to make long detours. You go and see the monuments. You count the churches, the equestrian statues, the public urinals, the Russian restaurants. You go and look at the major building works on the banks of the river, at the gates of the city, and the gutted streets that resemble ploughed fields, the pipe-laying, the blocks of flats being razed to the ground.

You go back to your room and collapse onto your too-narrow bed. You sleep, like a simpleton, with your eyes wide open. You count and you organise the cracks in the ceiling. The conjunction of shadows and stains, and the variations of adjustment and orientation of your gaze, produce effortlessly, slowly, dozens of nascent shapes, fragile coalitions that you are able to grasp only for a fleeting second, fixing them on a name: vine, virus, town, village, face, before they disintegrate and everything starts all over again: the sudden appearance of a gesture or move-ment, of an outline or the merest suggestion of an empty sign which you allow to develop, a chance meeting which grows into a firm acquaintance: an eye staring back at you, a man asleep, an eddy-pool, the gentle rocking of sail-boats, the tip of a tree, a branch shattered, preserved, recovered, and from which emerges with growing precision the beginnings of another face, hardly different from the last one, perhaps a little more grim or more attentive, a face in abeyance, in which you search in vain for the eyes, the neck, the forehead. But all that you are able to retain, or find, only to let slip again immediately, is the impression of an ambiguous smile, the shadow of a nostril, prolonged, perhaps, by the trace – ignominious or glorious, who can say? – of a scar.

You often play cards all by yourself. You deal out bridge hands, you try to solve the weekly problems in *Le Monde*, but you are no better than mediocre and your plays lack elegance: no subtlety in the squeeze, in the discards, in getting in and out of the dummy. One day you dreamt up a freak deal in which one pairing, having only two honours between them, an ace and a jack, could make a grand slam against any defence thanks to an unlikely distribution of chicanes and long suits. But then, once you'd perfected the problem and noticed that the slam in question was all the less interesting for being unbiddable, and that its execution did not involve a single finesse, you no longer had very high expectations of bridge.

You have fallen headlong into the spellbinding pleasures of patience. You deal out four columns of thirteen cards on the bed, you remove the four aces. The game consists in arranging the forty-eight remaining cards by using the four spaces left by the removal of the aces; if one of the spaces happens to be the first in a column, you are allowed to put a two there; if it follows, say, a six, you can insert the seven of the same suit, a seven can be followed by an eight, an eight by a nine, a jack by the queen; if the space follows a king, you may not lay anything and the space is dead.

Chance has virtually no role to play in this patience. You can foresee a long time in advance the moment when the four cleared spaces would bring you up against kings, and therefore failure, if you were to play them in order; but, precisely, you do not have to: you are allowed to use one space, then a different one, come back to the first, jump to the third, the fourth, back to the second again. Nevertheless, you rarely succeed; there always comes a point when the game is blocked, when, with half or a third of the cards already in order, you can no longer fill a space without turning up a king every time. In theory, you have the right to two more attempts: you just have to leave the ordered cards where they are and deal out again the other cards into four new columns, after having shuffled them. But you rarely avail yourself of these two supplementary chances; no sooner does the game appear lost than you scoop up all the cards, shuffle them once or twice, and deal them out again for another attempt.

You shuffle the cards, deal them out, remove the aces, and take stock of the situation. You begin more or less at random, taking care only to avoid laying bare a king too soon. Gradually, the game starts to take shape, constraints appear, possibilities come to light: there is one card already in its proper place, over here a single move will allow you to arrange five or six in one go, over there a king that is in your way cannot be moved.

You hardly ever get the patience out. You cheat sometimes, a little, rarely, increasingly rarely. Winning doesn't matter to you, for what would winning mean to you anyway, and if it's just a question of having the gods on your side, there are easier ways of inducing them to look kindly on you. But you play more and more often, for longer and longer, sometimes all afternoon, or as soon as you get up, or right through the night, and not even, not even any longer, just to kill time.

There is something about this game that fascinates you, perhaps even more than the game with the water under the bridges, or the labyrinths in the ceilings, or the imperfectly opaque twigs which drift slowly across the surface of your cornea. Depending on where it is, or when it crops up, each card acquires an almost poignant density. You protect, you destroy, you construct, you plot, you concoct one plan after another: a futile exercise, a danger that entails no risk of punishment, a derisory restoration of order: forty-eight cards keep you chained to your room and you feel almost happy when a ten happens to fall into place or when a king is unable to thwart you, and you feel almost unhappy when all your patient calculations lead to the same impossible outcome. It is as if this solitary silent strategy were your only way forward, as if it had become your reason for being.

IT'S DARK. The occasional car roars past in the street below. The drop of water forms on the tap on the landing. Your neighbour is silent, out perhaps, or dead already. You are stretched out on the bed, fully clothed, your hands crossed behind your neck and your knees up. You close your eyes, you open them. Viral, microbial forms, inside your eye, or on the surface of your cornea, drift slowly downwards, disappear, suddenly reappear in the centre, hardly changed, discs or bubbles, twigs, twisted filaments, which, when brought together, produce something resembling a barely mythological beast.

You lose track of them, then find them again; you rub your eyes and the filaments explode, proliferate.

Time passes, you are drowsy. You put down the open book beside you on the bed. Everything is vague, throbbing. Your breathing is astonishingly regular. A tiny, black insect, quite possibly unreal, opens up an undreamt-of breach in the labyrinth of cracks in the ceiling.

You drift around the streets, by night, by day. You go into local cinemas where the insistent stink of disinfectant hangs in the air, you eat sandwiches standing at the counter, chips in paper cones, you walk through fun-fairs, you play pinball, you go to museums, markets, stations, public libraries, you stare at the windows of the antique shops in

Rue Jacob, the glassware shops in Rue du Paradis, the furniture stores in Faubourg Saint-Antoine.

As the hours, the days, the weeks, the seasons slip by, you withdraw your affections, you detach yourself from everything. You discover, with something that sometimes almost resembles exhilaration, that you are free, that nothing is weighing you down, nothing pleases or displeases you. You find, in this life exempt from wear and tear and with no thrill in it other than these suspended moments that you procure through the playing cards, or certain noises, certain sights, an almost perfect, fascinating happiness, occasionally swollen by new emotions. You experience complete rest, at every moment you are spared, protected. You are living in a blessed parenthesis, in a vacuum full of promise, and from which you expect nothing. You are invisible, limpid, transparent. You no longer exist: across the passing hours, the succession of days, the procession of the seasons, the flow of time, you survive, without joy and without sadness, without a future and without a past, just like that: simply, self-evidently, like a drop of water forming on a drinking tap on a landing, like six socks soaking in a pink plastic bowl, like a fly or a mollusc, like a cow or a snail, like a child or an old man, like a rat.

SOMETIMES THE DARKNESS forms first the indistinct shape of an ace of spades: in front of you is a point from which two lines take off, move apart, and then come back in towards you after describing a long curve.

Later, it's an ocean, a black sea upon which you are sailing, as if your nose were the leading edge, or rather the stem of a gigantic ocean liner. Everything is black. It is not night-time, or heavily overcast, it is the whole world that is black, naturally black, like the negative of a photograph, and only the waves are white, or perhaps grey, the bow-waves thrown up on either side of your advancing nose, running the length of your eyes which are perhaps the sides of the ship, in the place where, previously, the ace of spades was inscribed, as if it had merely been the prelude to this wake, this off-white, undulating track that you cut before you as you slide through the black water. You are com-pletely surrounded by water, a black, motionless sea, as flat as a mill-pond, without the slightest phosphorescence, and yet you have the impression that you could discover every little detail, the slightest wisp of cloud if there were a sky, the tiniest dot of land if there were a horizon. But there is only the sea and you are nothing more than this stem, cutting effortlessly, silently, without vibration, the deep white traces of your passage, like a ploughshare furrowing a field.

Soon, however, somewhere above, as if on an inset map,

as if a cinema screen had appeared and the negative of a film were projected on to it, there is the same ship, but this time seen from above, in its entirety, and you are alone on deck, leaning on the ship's rail, or on the gunwale rather, striking a somewhat romantic pose. For a long time the impression of duplication remains quite precise, to the point where, if something is irritating you, nagging at you, it is that you are no longer able to distinguish between two alternatives: are you in the first instance the lone stem sliding over the black sea and throwing up white waves, and only subsequently, almost simultaneously, something resembling the consciousness of being this stem, that is to say, the ship, above, in its entirety and upon which you are the motionless passenger leaning on the deck, in a rather romantic pose? Or is it the other way round: is it the ship in its entirety that comes first, sliding over the black sea, with you, the lone passenger, leaning on the upper deck, and only then, enormously enlarged, a single detail of the ship, the stem, parting the seas, throwing up on either side two white waves, thick white waves that are perhaps a little too well delineated really to be waves, as if they were, rather, creases, the folds of a curtain, with something majestic about them, as if captured in slow motion?

For a long time the two ships, the part and the whole, your nose-stem and your body-liner, sail in convoy without your being able to separate them: you are at one and the same time the stem and the ship, and you on the ship. Then, a first contradiction arises, but it is perhaps just an optical illusion that could be ascribed to the disparity in scales, the difference in perpectives: it seems to you that the ship is slowing down, getting slower and slower, perhaps a little as though you were viewing it from further and further away, from an ever greater height, but you, at the same time, leaning on the ship's rail, you do not shrink in size at all, you remain just as visible; it seems also that the stem itself is accelerating, that it is no longer sliding, but skimming over the black water like a motor launch, like a speed-boat almost, and certainly no longer like a passenger liner.

But then – and this is straightaway far more serious, as if you knew by experience, perhaps, that what is taking shape is the beginning of the end, because you would never be able to stand for more than a couple of moments, a couple of seconds, the intensity of what is in the offing, although nothing has taken definite shape yet, apart from, perhaps, at the very most, a premonitory sign, a clue whose meaning was far from clear and whose explanation you now await in the vain hope that everything will remain vague as long as possible, because already, you know, a sudden awakening awaits you, indeed it is your very impatience that has set the process in motion and all your efforts to delay the moment serve only to hasten its arrival – but then, there emerges, like every other time, and not slowly enough, an impression which is at once exciting and tiresome, wondrous and appalling, straightaway too precise, very quickly obsessive and almost painful: the absurd certainty – well, not yet altogether absurd, but surely already destined to become so – that you have lived this image before, that it is a real memory, faithful in every respect: the sea was black, the ship advanced slowly down the narrow channel throwing up showers of white spume on either side, you were leaning against the rail of the walkway on the promenade deck in the rather romantic pose adopted by all passengers when they go up on deck to watch the sea-gulls, you felt precisely the same sensation that you feel now, and yet you no longer feel anything, except the perilous, the increasingly perilous sensation of knowing both the impossibility, and, at the same time, the irreducibility of such a memory.

*

Later, much later, perhaps you woke up and dozed off again several times, you turned onto your right side, onto your left side, onto your back, onto your front, perhaps you even switched on the light, perhaps you smoked a cigarette, later, much later, sleep becomes a target, or rather the reverse, it is you who become a target for sleep. It is a source of radiant, sporadic light. In front of you, or, to be more precise, before your eyes, sometimes a little to the left, other times more to the right, never in the centre, myriad tiny white dots begin to coalesce, forming at length something vaguely feline, a panther's head seen in profile, coming towards you, growing bigger and baring two sharp fangs, then disappearing and giving way to a luminous point which grows, turns into a lozenge, a star which hurtles towards you at great speed and misses you on the right at the very last moment. The phenomenon is repeated several times, regularly: nothing at first, then some faintly luminous dots, a panther's head which takes shape vaguely, becomes more precise, grows bigger and roars gapingly, baring two sharp fangs, then a shimmering, almost exploding, point of light which expands into the lozenge, the star, then the ball of light bearing down on you, passing by so close that you almost thought you had touched it, felt it, heard it, then nothing again, for a long time, white dots, the panther's head, the star that grows and whistles past your head.

Then nothing for a long time, or rather, later, sometimes, somewhere, something resembling a white star, which explodes . . .

IN THE COURSE OF TIME your coldness becomes awesome. Your eyes have lost the last vestige of their sparkle, your silhouette now slumps perfectly. An expression of serenity without lassitude, without bitterness, plays at the corners of your mouth. You slip through the streets, untouchable, protected by the judicious wear and tear of your clothing, by the neutrality of your gait. Now, your movements are simply acquired gestures. You utter only those words which are strictly necessary. You ask for:

- a coffee
- front of stalls
- the usual and a glass of red
- a beer
- a toothbrush
- a notebook

You pay, you pocket the change, you sit down, you eat. You take a copy of *Le Monde* from the top of its pile and place two twenty-centime coins in the vendor's dish. You never say please, hello, thank you, goodbye. You never say sorry. You do not ask your way.

You wander around, and around, and around. You walk. All moments are equivalent, all spaces are alike. You are never in a hurry, never lost. You do not look to see the time on the clocktowers. You are not sleepy. You are not hungry. You never yawn. You never burst into laughter.

You don't even stroll any more, since the only people who can stroll are those who snatch the time to do so, those who contrive to fiddle a few precious moments off their schedules. In the beginning you used to choose where you would go, you set goals for yourself, you devised complex itineraries, which, despite yourself, began to resemble the voyages of Ulysses. Like so many others before, you went on a pilgrimage to Saint-Julien-le-Pauvre, you walked round and round near the entrance to the Catacombs, you went and stood beneath the Eiffel Tower, you went up a few monuments, you crossed all the bridges, walked along all the embankments, visited all the museums, Guimet, Cernuschi, Carnavalet, Bourdelle, Delacroix, Nissim de Camondo, the Palais de la Découverte and the Aquarium du Trocadéro, you saw the rose gardens of Bagatelle, Montmartre by night, les Halles at first light, Saint-Lazare station in the rush-hour, Concorde at midday on August 15. But the fact that a given goal was trippery or cultural, disappointing or badly chosen, or even provocative (Rue de la Pompe, Rue des Saussaies, Place Beauvau, Quai des Orfèvres) did not stop it from being a goal, that is to say, a tension, an act of will, an emotion. Your tourism, even when it was disenchanted or derisory, and despite the distant memory of the Surrealists, was still a source of vigilance, a tabling of time, a measuring of space.

Just as you no longer choose your films, entering indiscriminately the first cinema you come to at around eight, nine or ten in the evening, the merest shadow of a spectator in the darkened auditorium, the shadow of a shadow watching as various combinations of shadow and light, form and dissolve on a rectangular oblong, ceaselessly sketching the same adventure: music, enchantment, suspense; just as you no longer choose your meals, as you no longer bother to vary them, to work your way right through the three hundred or so combinations that your five one-franc coins could procure for you at the counter of the Petite Source, those five one-franc coins which represent one third of your daily allowance, chinking in your pocket; just as you no longer choose when to sleep, or what to read, or what to wear . . .

You let yourself go, you allow yourself to be carried along: all it takes is for the crowd to be going up or going down the Champs Elysées, all it takes is for a grey back a few yards in front of you to turn off suddenly down a grey street; or else a light or an absence of light, a noise or an absence of noise, a wall, a group of people, a tree, some water, a porch, a fence, advertising posters, paving stones, a pedestrian crossing, a shopfront, a luminous stop/go sign, the name plate of a street, the red sign outside a tobacconist's, a haberdasher's stall, a flight of steps, a traffic island . . .

You walk or you do not walk. You sleep or you do not sleep. You walk down your six flights of stairs, you climb back up again. You buy *Le Monde* or you do not buy it. You eat or you do not eat. You sit down, you stretch out, you remain standing, you slip into the darkened auditorium of a cinema. You light a cigarette. You cross the street, you cross the Seine, you stop, you start again. You play pinball or you don't.

Sometimes, you stay in your room for three, four, five days at a time, you couldn't say for sure. You sleep almost uninterruptedly, you wash your socks, your two shirts. You reread a detective novel that you've already read, and forgotten, twenty times. You do the crossword in an old copy of *Le Monde* that you find lying around. You deal out on your bed four columns of thirteen cards, you remove the aces, you place the seven of hearts below the six of hearts, the two of spades in its space, the king of spades below the queen of spades, the jack of hearts below the ten of hearts.

You eat jam on bread, for as long as the bread lasts, then you spread it on crackers, if you have any, then you eat it straight from the jar on a spoon.

You stretch out on the narrow bed, hands crossed behind your neck, knees up. You close your eyes, you open them. Twisted filaments drift slowly down the surface of your cornea.
You count and organise the cracks, the flakes of paint and the flaws in the ceiling. You look at your face in the cracked mirror.

You don't talk to yourself, yet. You don't scream, especially not that.

Indifference has neither beginning nor end: it is an immutable state, a dead weight, an unshakeable inertia. Doubtless, messages from the outside world still make it through to your nerve centres, but no organised response involving the totality of the organism appears to be able to develop. All that remains are elementary reflexes: when the light is red you do not cross the road, you shelter from the wind in order to light a cigarette, you wrap up warmer on winter mornings, you change your sports shirt, your socks, your underpants and your vest about once a week, and your bed linen roughly every fortnight.
Indifference dissolves language and scrambles the signs. You are patient and you are not waiting, you are free and you do not choose, you are available and nothing arouses your enthusiasm. You ask for nothing. You demand nothing, you make no impositions. You hear without ever listening, you see without ever looking: the cracks in the

ceilings, in the floorboards, the patterns in the tiling, the lines around your eyes, the trees, the water, the stones, the cars passing in the street, the clouds that form . . . cloud shapes in the sky.

Now, your existence is boundless. Each day is made up of silence and noise, of light and blackness, layers, expectations, shivers. It is just a question of getting lost once again, for ever, more each time, of ceaseless wandering, of finding sleep, a certain physical calm: abandon, lassitude, drowsiness, drifting-off. You slide, you let yourself slip and go under: searching for emptiness, running from it. Walk, stop, sit down, take a table, lean on it, stretch out on your bed.

Robotic actions: get up, wash, shave, dress. A cork on the water: drift with the current, follow the crowd, trail about: in the heavy silence of summer, closed shutters, deserted streets, sticky asphalt, deathly-still leaves of a green that verges on black; in the cold light of the shop-fronts, the streetlights, the little clouds of condensing breath at café doors, the black stumps of the dead winter trees.

You frequent scruffy down-at-heel cafés, bistrots, back-street bars selling only wine by the glass, gloomy *Vins et Charbons* stinking of vinegar and accumulated filth. Out towards Charles Michels square or Château-Landon you walk down slimy alleyways, past hoardings disfigured by tattered posters. You sit on the benches in public gardens and parks, like a pensioner, an old man, but you are only twenty-five. You go and loiter in hotel lobbies, sitting on an imitation leather settee, you watch the people come and go, you read the brochures, catalogues, notices, you read the tourist leaflets. Paris by night, Cruise to the Indies, the glossy magazines that are lying around, the *Echo de l'Hôtellerie française*, the *Revue du Touring-Club de France*;

you go and read the newspapers displayed on boards outside printing works or editorial offices: *Le Monde*, *Le Figaro*,
Le Capital, *La Vie française*. You while away your time in
public libraries, you fill out a form, you read history books,
scholarly works, memoirs of statesmen, or mountaineers,
or parish priests.

You walk the streets, looking in the gutters or in the
space of variable width which separates the parked cars
from the kerbside. You discover marbles, little springs,
rings, coins, gloves, and on one occasion a wallet which
contained a little money, identity papers, letters, and some
photographs which almost made you cry.

You watch the card-players in the Luxembourg Gardens,
the great ornamental lakes of the Palais de Chaillot, on
Sundays you go to the Louvre, walking straight through
all the rooms and finally stationing yourself in front of a
single painting or a single object: the unbelievably energetic
portrait of a Renaissance man with a tiny scar above his
upper lip, on the left, that is to say to his left, your right,
or perhaps a stone engraving, or else a small Egyptian
spoon in front of which you stand for an hour, or two
hours, before leaving without looking back.

It is one ceaseless and untiring circumambulation. You
walk like someone carrying invisible suitcases, like
someone following his own shadow. A blind man, a
sleepwalker. You proceed with a mechanical tread, never-
endingly, to the point where you even forget that you are
walking.

You are a meticulous stroller, an accomplished nightowl,
a blob of ectoplasm, which, with the addition of a billowing
sheet, could be mistaken for a ghost incapable of scaring
even tiny children.

You are a tireless walker: every evening you emerge
from the black hole of your room, from your rotting

staircase, your silent courtyard, to criss-cross Paris; beyond the great pools of noise and light: Opéra, the Boulevards, the Champs Elysées, Saint-Germain, Montparnasse, you head out towards the dead city, towards Péreire or Saint-Antoine, towards Rue de Longchamp, Boulevard de l'Hôpital, Rue Oberkampf, Rue Vercingétorix.

All-night cafés. You remain standing, almost motionless, with one elbow resting on the glass counter – a thick, translucent sheet with rounded edges, fixed to its concrete base by means of copper bolts – half-turned towards a pinball machine into which three sailors shovel endless coins. You drink red wine or percolated coffee.

It is a life without surprises. You are safe. You sleep, you walk, you continue to live, like a laboratory rat abandoned in its maze by some absent-minded scientist, and which, morning and night, unerringly, unhesitatingly, follows the path to its food dispenser, turning left, turning right, pressing down twice on a pedal ringed in red in order to receive its portion of homogenised feed.

There is no hierarchy, no preference. Your indifference is motionless, becalmed: a grey man for whom grey has no connotation of dullness. Not insensitive but neutral. You are attracted by water, but also by stone; by darkness, but also by light; by warmth, but also by cold. All that exists is your walking, and your gaze, which lingers and slides, oblivious to beauty, to ugliness, to the familiar, the surprising, only ever retaining combinations of shapes and lights, which form and dissolve continuously, all around you, in your eyes, on the ceilings, at your feet, in the sky, in your cracked mirror, in the water, in the stone, in the crowds. Squares, avenues, parks and boulevards, trees and railings, men and women, children and dogs, queues, crushes, vehicles and shop windows, buildings, façades, columns and capitals, pavements, gutters, sandstone paving flags glistening grey in the drizzle, or almost red, or almost white, or almost black, or almost blue. Silences, rows, rackets, crowds at the stations, in the shops, on the boulevards, teeming streets, packed platforms, deserted Sunday streets in August, mornings, evenings, nights, dawns and dusks.

Now you are the nameless master of the world, the one on whom history has lost its hold, the one who no longer feels the rain falling, who does not see the approach of night.

All you are is all you know: your life that continues, your breathing, your step, your ageing. You see the people coming and going, crowds and objects taking shape and dissolving. Your eye is suddenly caught by a curtain rail in the tiny window of a haberdasher's: you continue on your way: you are inaccessible.

A MOUNTAIN IS ENGENDERED by the meeting of your eye and the pillow, a fairly gentle slope, a segment, or rather the arc of a circle which stands out in the foreground, darker than the rest of the space. This mountain is not worth bothering with; it is quite unexceptional. For the moment, your mind is preoccupied with a task that you somehow feel you should accomplish but which you are unable to define precisely; a task of little importance in itself but which is, perhaps, merely the pretext, the opportunity, to check whether you know the code; you suppose, for example, and this is immediately confirmed, that the task consists in drawing your thumb, or the whole of your hand, up over the pillow: but is it really your job to do this? Should you not be exempted from this tedious chore by virtue of your position in the hierarchy and your years of service? This problem is clearly a lot more important than the task itself, and you have no means of solving it, since you never dreamt that after so long you would still be called to account in this manner. And what is more, when you come to think about it, the problem is even more complicated: it is not a question of knowing whether or not you should move your thumb in accordance with your function, your grade, your seniority, but rather this: you will have to move your thumb sooner or later in any case, but you will lift it *over* the pillow if you are senior enough, and slide it *under* the pillow if you are not, and naturally you have no idea as to how many years of service you have, except that you feel you have a considerable number, though perhaps not considerable enough. Perhaps they even chose this moment to pose the question precisely because it is the very moment when nobody, not even the most honest and upstanding judge, would be able to declare with certainty that you are, or are not, sufficiently senior?

The question could apply equally well to your feet or your thighs. In fact, the question is meaningless: the real problem revolves around contact. In theory, there are two kinds of contact: the contact of your body with the sheets, and this applies to your left thigh, your right foot, your right forearm, part of your stomach: this contact is fusion, osmosis, dilution; and the contact of your body with itself, in those places where flesh meets flesh, where your left foot rests on your right foot, where your knees meet, where your elbow comes up against your stomach: these contacts are sharp, hot or cold, or both hot and cold. One could naturally, and almost without risk, invert the whole operation and maintain that it is the other way round, the left foot under the right foot, the right thigh under the left thigh.

What emerges most clearly from all of this is obviously that you are not lying down on your right or your left side, with your legs slightly bent and your arms wrapped around the pillow, but hanging upside-down, like a hibernating bat, or, rather, an over-ripe pear on a pear-tree: this means you could fall at any moment, although you are not overly alarmed by the prospect since your head is perfectly protected by the pillow, but it is nevertheless your duty to avoid this danger, no matter how slight it may be. But if you run through in your head all the means that you know of, you soon realise that the situation is more serious than you had initially imagined, if only because the loss of horizontality is rarely conducive to sleep. So, you will have to resign yourself to falling, even though you foresee that it will not be particularly pleasant (one never knows when one will stop falling), but above all, you do not know how to go about letting yourself fall, it's only when you are not thinking about it that you start falling, and how could you not think about it since, precisely, you are thinking about it? That is something that no-one has ever given serious thought to, but which is not without a certain importance: there should be books written about it, reliable books that would enable one to face up to these situations which occur far more often than is generally thought.

Three-quarters of your body has taken refuge in your head; your heart has taken up residence in your eyebrow where it now feels quite at home, where it is beating like a living creature, albeit, perhaps, at the very most, a little too quickly. You will have to conduct a roll-call of your body, to check that your limbs, your organs, your entrails, your mucous membranes are all intact. You would really like to clear your head of all these pieces that are cluttering it up and weighing it down, but at the same time, you congratulate yourself on having saved as much as you could, for everything else is lost, you no longer have any feet, or hands, your calf-muscle has turned to jelly.

This is all becoming increasingly complicated: what you should do first is to remove your elbow, and then, in the space that is thus created, you could place at least a portion of your tummy, and so on until you are more or less back together again. But it is terribly difficult: there are bits missing, others are duplicated, others still have grown outrageously large, and yet others are voicing utterly insane territorial claims: your elbow is more an elbow than ever, you had forgotten just how elbow-like an elbow could be, a fingernail has supplanted your whole hand. And this, naturally, is always the moment that the torturers choose to intervene. One of them stuffs a chalk-filled sponge into your mouth, another bungs up your ears with cotton wool; a few pit-sawyers have set to work in your sinus passages, a pyromaniac is on the loose in your stomach, sadistic tailors compress your feet, force your head into a hat which is too small, cram you into an overcoat that is too tight, strangle you with a necktie; a sweep and his sidekick have introduced a knotted rope into your windpipe and, despite their best efforts, are unable to withdraw it.

They come almost every time. You know them well. It is almost reassuring. If they have arrived, it means that sleep cannot be too far off. They will make you suffer a little, then they'll get bored and leave you alone. They hurt you, that goes without saying, but you have, with regard to pain, as with all the sensations you perceive, all the thoughts that cross your mind, all the impressions you feel, an attitude of complete detachment. You see yourself without astonishment being astonished, without surprise being surprised, without pain being assaulted by the torturers. You wait for them to calm down. You willingly concede to them whatever organs they want. You watch them from afar arguing over your stomach, your nose, your throat, your feet.

But often, so often, this is just the final snare. Then the worst begins. It wells up slowly, imperceptibly. At first everything is calm, too calm, normal, too normal. Everything looks as if it will never have to move again. But then you know, you begin to know, with ever more implacable certainty, that you have lost your body, or no . . . it is rather that you can see it, not far away, but you will never again be able to get back to it.

You are now nothing more than an eye. A huge staring

eye which sees everything, which sees your limp body just as it sees you, looked at and looking, as if it had turned round completely in its socket and was contemplating you in silence, you, the inside of you, the dark, empty, slime-green, frightened, impotent interior of you. It looks at you and it nails you to the spot. You will never stop seeing yourself. You can do nothing, you cannot escape yourself, you cannot escape your own gaze, you never will be able to: even if you were to fall into a sleep so deep that no shock, no shout, no burning pain could rouse you, there would still be this eye, your eye, that will never close, that will never sleep.

You see yourself, you see yourself seeing yourself, you watch yourself watching yourself. Even if you were to wake up, your vision would remain the same, immutable. Even if you managed to grow thousands, billions of extra eyelids, there would still be this eye, behind, which would see you. You are not asleep but sleep will never come again. You are not awake and you will never wake up. You are not dead and even death could never set you free.

As free as a cow, as a mollusc, as a rat!

But rats don't spend hours trying to get to sleep. But rats don't wake up with a start, gripped by panic, bathed in sweat. But rats don't dream and what can you do to protect yourself against your dreams?

But rats don't bite their nails, especially not methodically, for hours on end, until the tips of their claws are little more than a large open sore. You tear off half of the nail, bruising the spots where it is attached to the flesh; you tear away the cuticle nearly all the way back to the top joint until beads of blood start to appear, until your fingers are so painful that, for hours, the slightest contact is so unbearable that you can no longer pick things up and you have to go and immerse your hands in scalding hot water.

But rats, as far as you know, do not play pinball. You hug the machines for hours on end, for nights on end, feverishly, angrily. You cling, grunting, to the machines, accompanying the erratic rebounds of the steel ball with exaggerated thrusts of your hips. You wage relentless warfare on the springs, the lights, the figures, the channels. Painted ladies who give an electronic wink, who lower their fans. You can't fight against a tilt. You can play or not play. You can't start up a conversation, you can't make it say what it will never be able to say to you. It is no use snuggling up close to it, panting over it, the tilt remains insensitive to the friendship you feel, to the love which you seek, to the desire which torments you. Six thousand points, when four thousand four hundred are enough for a replay, will only add to your bruises, will only beat you down a little further.

You drift around the streets, you enter a cinema; you drift around the streets, you enter a bar; you drift around the streets, you look at the Seine, the butchers' shops, the trains, the posters, people. You drift around the streets, you enter a cinema where you see a film which resembles the one you've just seen, the same inane story, full of sweetness and music, told by a gentleman who is too intelligent to be real, then the intermission, commercials that you've seen ten, twenty times, a documentary about sardines, or the sun, about Hawaii or the *Bibliothèque Nationale*, a trailer for a film you've already seen and will see again, the film that you've just watched starting all over again, with its fragmented title-sequence, the beach at Etretat, sea, sea-gulls, children playing in the sand.

You walk out, you drift around the over-lit streets. You go back to your room, you undress, you slip between the sheets, you turn out the light, you close your eyes. Now is the time when dream-women, too quickly undressed, crowd in around you, the time when you reread *ad nauseam* books you've read a hundred times before, when you toss and turn for hours without getting to sleep. This is the hour when, your eyes wide open in the darkness, your hand groping towards the foot of the narrow bed in search of an ashtray, matches, a last cigarette, you calmly measure the sticky extent of your unhappiness.

Now you get up in the night. You wander the streets, you go and perch on bar-stools at the Rosebud, at Harry's Bar, or take a seat at the Franco-Suisse in Rue Saint-Honoré, almost directly across the street from your room, or you install yourself at a café table in Les Halles, and there you stay, for hours, until closing-time, with a beer in front of you or a black coffee or a glass of red wine. You watch the others come and go, the butcher's boys, the florists, the newspaper vendors, the crowds of merry revellers, the lonely boozers, the tarts.

You are alone and drifting. You walk along the desolate avenues, past the stunted trees, the peeling façades, the dark porches. You penetrate the bottomless ugliness of Les Batignolles, and Pantin. Your only chance encounters are with Wallace fountains which long since ran dry, tacky churches, gutted building sites, pale walls. The parks whose railings imprison you, the festering swamps near the sewer outlets, the monstrous factory gates. Steam locomotives pump out clouds of white smoke under the metallic walkways of the area around Gare Saint-Lazare. On Boulevard Barbès or Place Clichy, impatient crowds raise their eyes to the heavens.

You will not break the magic circle of solitude. You are alone and you know no-one; you know no-one and you are alone. You see the others bunch together, huddle together, hug and protect one other. But you, lifeless gaze, transparent wraith, leper blending with the walls, you are a silhouette already returned to dust, an occupied space that no-one approaches. You force yourself to hope for unlikely encounters. But it is not for you that leather, brass and wood start suddenly to shine, that lights are lowered and noises gently muffled. You are alone despite the thickening cigarette smoke, despite Lester Young or Coltrane, alone in the snug heat of the bars, in the empty streets which echo to your tread, in the drowsy complicity of the last bars to remain open.

There are some enemies that you will face up to only

once, just long enough to know, to recognise, the icy hiss of the snake which would turn you to stone, just long enough to beat a timely retreat, chilled with loneliness and impatience, done for, betrayed by your own eyes, by the ever sharper and ever more futile perception of the tiniest details: a curl of hair, the shadow of a glass, the shifting outline of a discarded cigarette, the final tremor of a closing double-door. You miss nothing, but neither do you grasp anything, or if you do it is too late, always too late: shadows, reflections, cracks, sidesteps, smiles, yawns, tiredness or abandon.

Unhappiness did not swoop down on you, this was no surprise attack: more of a gradual infiltration, it insinuated itself almost ingratiatingly. It meticulously impregnated your life, your movements, the hours you keep, your room, like a long-obscured truth, or something that was staring you in the face but which you refused to recognise; tenacious and patient, subtle and unremitting, it took possession of the cracks in the ceiling, of the lines in your face in the cracked mirror, of the pack of cards; it slipped furtively into the dripping tap on the landing, it echoed in sympathy with the chimes of each quarter-hour from the bells of Saint-Roch.

The snare was that feeling which, on occasion, came close to exhilaration, that arrogance, that sort of exaltation; you thought that the city was all you needed, its stones and its streets, the crowds which carried you along, a tiny space on the counter at the Petite Source, a front of stalls in some local cinema; you thought you needed only your room, your lair, your cage, your burrow, to which you return each day, from which you set out again each day, this almost magical place which no longer contains anything to occupy your patience, not even a crack in the ceiling, not even a feature of the grain in the wood of your shelf, not even a flower in the patterned wallpaper. Once again you deal out the fifty-two cards on your narrow bed; once again you search for the unlikely exit from a shapeless labyrinth.

Your powers have deserted you. You no longer know how to follow the lazy drift of the bubbles and twigs over the surface of your cornea. You are no longer able to summon up a face, a triumphal cavalcade or a distant city out of the cracks and the shadows.

The snare: the dangerous illusion of being – what is the word? – impenetrable, of offering no purchase to the outside world, of silently sliding, inaccessible, just two open eyes looking forward, perceiving everything, the tiniest details, retaining nothing. Like a sleepwalker who is wide awake, or a blindman who can see. A being without memory, without alarm.

But there is no exit, no miracle, no truth. Shells, protective armour. Ever since that stifling day when it all started, when everything stopped. You hug the filthy walls of the black streets, your right hand knocking against the porch-steps, the bricks of the façades. Sitting for hours above the Seine, your legs dangling, you contemplate the scarcely perceptible eddy caused by the arch of a bridge. You withdraw the four aces from your fifty-two cards. How many times have you repeated the same amputated gestures, the same journeys which lead nowhere? All you have left to fall back on are your tuppeny-halfpenny bolt-holes, your idiotic patience, the thousand and one detours that always lead you back unfailingly to your starting point. From park to museum, from café to cinema, from embankment to garden, the station waiting-rooms, the lobbies of the grand hotels, the supermarkets, the book-shops, the art galleries, the corridors of the metro. Trees, stones, water, clouds, sand, brick, light, wind, rain: all that counts is your solitude: whatever you do, wherever you go, nothing that you see has any importance, nothing that you seek is real, everything that you do, you do in vain. Inviting or calamitous, solitude alone exists, this solitude with which, sooner or later, every time, you are confronted; every time, you face it alone and defenceless, raging or distraught, in despair or impatient.

You stopped speaking and only silence replied. But those words, those thousands, those millions of words that dried up in your throat, the inconsequential chit-chat, the cries of joy, the words of love, the silly laughter, just when will you find them again?

Now you live in dread of silence. But are you not the most silent of all?

The monsters have come into your life, the rats, your fellow creatures, your brothers. The monsters in their tens, their hundreds, their thousands. You can spot them from almost subliminal signs, from their silences, their furtive departures, from their shifty, hesitant, startled eyes that look away when they meet yours. In the middle of the night a light still shows at the attic windows of their sordid little rooms. Their footfalls echo in the night.

The rats don't speak to each other or look at each other when they meet. But you can sense these eyeless faces, these frail or drooping figures, these hunched, grey backs, you can feel their constant proximity, you follow their shadows, you are their shadow, you frequent their hide-outs, their pokey little holes, you have the same refuges, the same sanctuaries: the local cinema which stinks of disinfectant, the public gardens, the museums, the cafés, the stations, the metro, the covered markets. Bundles of despair sitting like you on park benches, endlessly drawing and rubbing out the same imperfect circle in the sand, readers of newspapers found in rubbish bins, wanderers who wander come rain or storm. They follow the same circuits as you, just as futile, just as slow, just as desperately byzantine. Like you, they hesitate in front of the maps in the metro, they eat their buns sitting on the river banks.

The exiles, the banished, the pariahs, the wearers of invisible stars. When they walk, they hug the walls, eyes cast down and shoulders drooping, clutching at the stones of the façades, with the weary gestures of a defeated army, of those who bite the dust.

You follow them, you spy on them, you hate them: monsters in their garrets, monsters in slippers who shuffle at the fringes of the putrid markets, monsters with dead fish-eyes, monsters moving like robots, monsters who drivel.

You rub shoulders with them, you walk with them, you make your way amongst them: the sleepwalkers, the animals, the old men, the cretins, the deaf-mutes with their berets pulled down over their ears, the drunkards, the dotards who clear their throats and try to control the spasms of their cheek muscles or the twitching of their eyelids, the peasants lost in the big city, the widows, the slyboots, the old boys, the snoopers.

They came to you, they grabbed you by the arm. As if, because you are a stranger lost in your own city, you could only meet other strangers; as if, because you are alone, you had to watch as all the other loners swooped down on you. As if only those who never speak, those who talk to themselves, could ever meet up, just for the time it takes to drink a glass of red wine at the same bar. The old lunatics, the old lushes, the cranks, the exiles. They button-hole you, they hang on to your coat tails and your cuffs, they breathe in your face.

They sidle up to you with their wholesome smiles, their leaflets, their newspapers, their flags, the pathetic champions of great lost causes, the bony masks crusading against poliomyelitis, cancer, slum housing, poverty, hemiplegia, blindness, the sad *chansonniers* out collecting for their friends, the abused orphans selling table-mats, the scraggy widows who protect pets. All those who accost you, detain you, paw you, ram their petty-minded truth down your throat, spit their eternal questions in your face, belabour you with their charitable works and their True Way. The sandwich-men of the true faith which will save the world. Come unto Him all ye who suffer. Jesus said: if ye were blind, ye should have no sin.

The sallow complexions, the frayed collars, the stammerers who tell you their life story, who tell you about their time in prison, in the asylum, in the hospital, their imagined voyages. The old school teachers who have a plan to standardise spelling, the pensioners who think they've devised a foolproof system for recyling old paper, the strategists, the astrologers, the water diviners, the faith healers, the witnesses, all those who live with their obsessions; the failures, the dead beats, the harmless and senile monsters mocked by bartenders who fill their glasses so high that they can't raise them to their lips, the old bags in their furs who try to remain dignified whilst knocking back the Marie Brizard.

And all the others who are even worse, the smug, the smart-Alecs, the self-satisfied, those who think they know a thing or two and who smile in a knowing sort of way, the fat men and the forever young, the dairymen and the decorated; the revellers on a binge, the Brylcreem-boys from the suburbs, the stinking rich, the dumb bastards. The monsters confident of their own rights, who address you without further ado, call you to witness, stare you out. The monsters with their big families, with their monster children and their monster dogs; the thousands of monsters caught at the traffic lights; the yapping females of the monsters; the monsters with moustaches, and waistcoats, and braces, the tourist monsters tipped out by the coachload in front of the hideous monuments, the monsters in their Sunday best, the monstrous crowd.

You drift around, but the crowd no longer carries you, the night no longer protects you. Still you walk, ever onwards, untiring, immortal. You search, you wait. You wander through the fossilised town, the intact white stones of the restored façades, the petrified dustbins, the vacant chairs where concierges once sat; you wander through the ghost town, scaffolding abandoned against gutted apartment blocks, bridges adrift in the fog and the rain.

Putrid city, vile, repulsive city. Sad city, sad lights in the sad streets, sad clowns in the sad music-halls, sad queues outside the sad cinemas, sad furniture in the sad stores. Dark stations, barracks, warehouses. The gloomy bars which line the Grands Boulevards, the ugly shopfronts. Noisy or deserted city, pallid or hysterical city, gutted, devastated, soiled city, city bristling with prohibitions, steel bars, iron fences, locks. Charnel house city: the covered markets that are rotting away, the shanty towns disguised as housing projects, the slum belt in the heart of Paris, the unbearable horror of the boulevards where the cops hang out: Haussmann, Magenta—and Charonne.

Like a prisoner, like a madman in his cell. Like a rat looking for the way out of his maze. You pace the length and breadth of Paris. Like a starving man, like a messenger delivering a letter with no address.

You wait, you hope. Dogs have grown attached to you, so have barmaids, café waiters, usherettes, cinema box-office ladies, newspaper vendors, bus conductors, the war veterans who watch over the empty rooms in museums. You can speak freely, they will always answer you in the same measured tone. Their faces are now familiar to you. They identify you, recognise you. They do not realise that these simple daily greetings, these mere smiles, these indifferent nods are all that keeps your head above water; nor do they know that you have been waiting all day for them, as if they were the reward for some heroic deed that you are not at liberty to talk about, but which they have somehow divined anyway.

So, occasionally, you attempt in desperation to impose a rigid discipline on your faltering existence. You bring a little order into your life, you tidy up your room, you draw up a strict budget: your monthly allowance of 500 francs, less 50 francs for your room, leaves you 15 francs a day, which breaks down in the following way:

a packet of gauloises	1,35
a box of matches	0,10
a meal	4,20
a cinema ticket	2,50
a tip for the usherette	0,20
Le Monde	0,40
a coffee	1,00

You have 5,25 francs left for your second meal – which will be a raisin bun or half a baguette – for another coffee, for the metro, the bus, some toothpaste, the laundry.

You set your life like a watch, as if the best means of saving yourself, of avoiding going under altogether, were to set yourself derisory tasks, to decide everything in advance, to leave nothing to chance. Let your life be closed, smooth, rounded and full, let your actions be dictated by a fixed, immutable order which decides everything on your behalf, which protects you against yourself.

You establish your itineraries with commendable thoroughness. You explore Paris street by street, from Montsouris park to the Buttes-Chaumont, from the Palais de la Défense to the War Ministry, from the Eiffel tower to the Catacombs. You eat the same meal, at the same time, every day. You visit the stations and the museums. You drink your coffee in the same café. From five until seven you read *Le Monde*.

You fold up your clothes before getting into bed. On Saturday mornings you clean your room thoroughly. You make your bed every morning, you shave, you wash your socks in a pink plastic bowl, you polish your shoes, you brush your teeth, you wash up your coffee bowl, dry it, and place it in the same spot on the shelf. Every morning you remove, at the same time, in the same place, in the same way, the gummed paper seal from your daily packet of gauloises.

The orderliness of your room. The regularity of your timetable. You impose childish constraints on yourself. You do not step on the cracks between the paving slabs near the kerbside, you go the right way around traffic islands, you observe parking restrictions. You cannot stand being late or early. You would like to light your cigarettes at intervals of precisely forty-five minutes.

It is as if you were living with the constant dread that the slightest weakening of your resolution might, all at once, take you too far.

It is as if you constantly needed to tell yourself: it is this way because I wanted it this way, I wanted it this way, otherwise I am dead.

SOMETIMES YOU SPEND whole evenings listening to the comings and goings of your neighbour, half stretched-out on your narrow bed, with no other light than that which filters through your garret window, pale and diffuse, augmented only, and at almost regular intervals, by the glowing tip of a cigarette. The partition wall that separates your two rooms is so thin that you can almost hear him breathing, that you can still hear him even when he is shuffling around in his slippers. You often try to imagine what he looks like, his face, his hands, what he does for a living, his age, his opinions. You know nothing about him, you've never even seen him, or perhaps, once at most, when you bumped into him on the stairs, squashing up against the wall to let him pass, but without knowing at that time, without being certain, that it was indeed him. And in any case, you do not try to catch a glimpse of him, you do not open your door a crack when you hear him going out onto the landing to fill his kettle from the tap, you prefer to listen to him and to be free to imagine him as you wish. You know only that his room is much bigger than yours, since he can move around in it, since he has to move in order to get to the window, or the bed, or the door, or the wardrobes; whereas, from the centre of your room, at a point about three quarters of the way down your bed, you are able, keeping your feet together, to touch any part of it: the window, the door, the wash basin, the alcove where you hang your clothes, the pink plastic bowl, the shelf.

He must be old, judging from his rather chesty cough, the rattle of his throat, the way he drags his feet. Not that it is even necessary to put down his solitary lifestyle to old age (like you, he never has any visitors to his room, as if the top floor of the apartment block, of which you two, as far as you know, are the only occupants, had recently come to represent some kind of threat to the safety of those who might once have been tempted to venture up there), nor is old age necessarily the explanation for the obsessively regular hours that he keeps. The latter would rather tend to suggest that he is, again a little like you, a creature of set habits, but, if that is the case, he is probably easier in his mind than you. He leaves his room every day, even on Sundays, just before lunchtime, and returns regularly at nightfall, as if his occupation, whether gainful or not, were determined by the hours of daylight rather than by the hours of the clock: he returned a little earlier each day until Christmas, now he comes back each day a little later.

You think he might be a street-vendor selling neckties displayed in an open umbrella, or, more likely, a demonstrator for some miracle product which removes corns, stains, warts or varicose veins, or, better still, a small-time haberdasher whose stall, consisting of an open suitcase resting on four telescopic legs, tempts the passers-by on the Grands Boulevards with combs, lighters, nail-files, sunglasses, protective cases, key-rings. This supposition is largely based on the fact that his main activity, when he is in his room, morning and evening, consists in closing and opening, or opening and closing, drawers, as if he had a considerable amount of material to get together each morning before he goes out, and to put away each evening at the end of his day.

Perhaps he needs his open suitcase, perhaps he uses it as

a bedside table, or to write on, or to eat his meals off: you deck him out with an array of somewhat ceremonious, and faintly ridiculous, characteristics: on his suitcase he lays out an embroidered tablecloth, the last vestige of a vanished fortune, a shoddy candelabrum set with cheap candles, a dinner service identical to the ones he may sell, consisting, that is to say, of a beaker and a plate in pink plastic, and a set of aluminium cutlery whose pieces all fit inside one another, the spoon bearing the hollow imprint of the fork, and the fork that of the knife, the three pieces being held together by a rivet in the form of an elongated collar stud fixed to the spoon and passing through the fork and knife, and to which a leather band is attached; all in all, it is as if, through some strange confusion in your mind, this suitcase, whose very existence is at best only hypothetical, could be at one and the same time a haberdasher's stall during the day, and a picnic basket in the evening. But it is not even certain that your neighbour dines in his room: you never hear, or smell, the sizzling giblets and kidneys which you imagine to be his favourite food. All that you know with any degree of certainty is that he goes and fills his kettle from the tap on the landing (for although his room is bigger than yours, it still doesn't have drinking water), and that he places it on a hotplate, whose mode of operation is unknown to you, but which is doubtless of a rather primitive variety, given the time it takes for the kettle to start whistling, that is to say, for the water to boil.

You may well listen, prick up your ears, press them against the wall, but when all is said and done you know next to nothing. It seems that your confidence in your interpretations diminishes in inverse proportion to the precision of your perceptions. Certainly, he opens and closes drawers all the time, but even that isn't proven, it is not entirely out of the question, for example, that for some reason best known to him, he is rubbing together two pieces of wood, or that he is indeed opening and closing one or several drawers, but for no particular reason, that is to say, without putting anything in or taking anything out, simply for the sake of making some noise, or because he likes the sound of opening and closing drawers. Certainly, he goes out every day shortly before lunchtime, but you are not always there to verify this, and, by the same token, you sometimes go out when it gets dark, and before he returns home; perhaps he even knows how to fake a departure: going down a few steps then creeping back up so softly that, despite all your efforts, you are no longer able to detect his presence. Certainly, he draws water from the tap on the landing, certainly his kettle whistles when the water reaches boiling point, but perhaps it is he who is whistling – there is no way of knowing.

And yet, occasionally, his life belongs to you, his noises are yours, since you are listening, waiting for them, since they keep you alive, like the dripping tap, like the bells of Saint-Roch, or the noises of the street, the sounds of the city. It doesn't really matter if you are wrong, if you are interpreting, inventing. It is sufficient that you have made him into a haberdasher for him to be one, with his folding suitcase, his combs, his lighters, his sunglasses. He leads the slender existence that you allow him to lead, fading away the moment he leaves the range of your perception, dead as soon as you drop off to sleep, condemned the rest of the time to fill his kettle, cough, drag his feet, open and close his drawers.

But perhaps unwittingly, by some silent symbiosis, you also belong to him? Perhaps he is like you – as you listen out for his cough, the whistling, the noises of his drawers

– perhaps the noise of your cup as you replace it on the shelf, the rustling of the newspapers that you pick up and put down, the slithering of the cards that you deal out onto your narrow bed, the noise of running water, your breathing, perhaps all of this, along with the dripping tap, the belltower, the noises of the streets, the sounds of the city, constitutes for him the tightly-woven fabric of passing time, of the life that remains. Perhaps he is trying desperately to know you, perhaps he endlessly interprets every sign he perceives: who are you, what do you do, you who rustle newspapers, you who stay in for several days at a time, or stay out for several days without coming home?

But you make so little noise! He can at most detect your presence, and, if he pays so much attention to it, it must be because he is afraid, because you worry him: he is like that old badger in his burrow that can never be too well protected, who can hear somewhere close-by a noise that he never succeeds in pinning down, a noise which never grows any louder, never grows any softer, never ceases. He tries to protect himself, he makes clumsy attempts to set snares for you, to make you believe that he is strong, that he is not afraid of you, that he is not quaking: but he is so old! What little strength he has left is employed in endlessly counting his fortune, in continually changing its hiding place.

Sometimes, you quite like to believe, you fool, that you fascinate him, that he really is afraid: you try to remain silent for as long as possible; or you take a piece of wood, or a nailfile, or a pencil, and scratch the top of the partition that separates your two rooms, producing a tiny, irritating noise.

*

Or else, in a sudden rush of sympathy, you almost feel like sending him salutary messages, tapping with your fist against the partition, one knock for A, two knocks for B . . .

Now you have run out of hiding places. You are afraid and you are waiting for everything to stop, the rain, the hours, the stream of traffic, life, people, the world; waiting for everything to collapse, walls, towers, floors and ceilings; waiting for men and women, old people and children, dogs, horses, birds, to fall, one by one, to the ground, paralysed, plague-ridden, epileptic; waiting for the marble to crumble away, for the wood to turn to pulp, for the houses to collapse noiselessly, for diluvian rains to dissolve the paintwork, pull apart the dowel-joints in hundred-year-old wardrobes, tear fabrics to shreds, wash away the newspaper ink; waiting for a fire without flames to consume the stairs; waiting for the streets to subside and split down the middle to reveal the gaping labyrinth of the sewers; waiting for rust and mist to invade the city.

Sometimes, you dream that sleep is a slow death creeping up on you, an anaesthesia at once sweet and fearful, a blissful necrosis: the chill climbs gradually up your legs, up your arms, numbing you slowly, slowly wiping you out. Your toe is a distant peak, your leg is a river, your cheek is your pillow, you are residing wholly in your thumb, you melt, you flow like sand, like mercury. You are nothing more than a grain of sand, a curled-up homunculus, a tiny blob, without muscles, without bones, without legs, without arms, without a neck, feet and hands merged into one, enormous lips swallowing you up.

You grow enormously, you explode, you die, you are crazed, petrified: your knees are hard stones, your tibias are steel bars, your stomach is an ice-floe, your penis is an oven, your heart a cauldron. Your head is a mist-shrouded moor, thin veils, thick blankets, heavy cloaks . . .

Your eyebrows lift and narrow, your brow is able to furrow, your eyes stare back at you. Your mouth opens and closes.

You study yourself carefully in the mirror and, even when you look closely, you look much more fair of face than you thought you were (although, in all truth, it is the light of evening and the source of light is behind you, so that only the fine fluff which covers the rim of your ears is properly lit). It is a pure, harmoniously proportioned face, almost handsome in its outlines. The black of the hair, the eyebrows and the eye sockets leaps out at you like a living creature against the mass of the face which is as yet undecided. The expression of the eyes is in no way ravaged by time, which has left no trace there, but it is not childlike either: it is, if anything, unbelievably energetic, unless, of course, it is merely observant, since you are, precisely, in the act of observing yourself, and trying to frighten yourself.

What secrets do you expect to find in your cracked mirror? And what truth in your face? This slightly swollen moon-shaped face, already somewhat puffy, these eyebrows which meet in the middle, that tiny scar over your lip, those somewhat protuberant eyes, those uneven teeth, covered in yellowish tartar, that mass of excrescences, spots, naevi, blackheads, warts, comedos, blackish or brownish moles with a few hairs growing out of them, under the eyes, on the nose, below the temples. By moving up very close you are able to discover that your skin is astonishingly furrowed, lined, scoured. You can see every pore, every swelling. You look, you scrutinise the wings of your nose, the cracks in your lips, the roots of your hair, the burst blood vessels which streak the whites of your eyes with red.

Sometimes, you look like a cow. Your protuberant eyes register no interest in what they see. You see yourself in the mirror and what you see arouses no feelings in you, not even such as might arise from simple familiarity. This somewhat bovine reflection, which you have learnt from experience to identify as the surest image of your face, appears to bear no trace of sympathy for you, of recognition, as if, indeed, it didn't recognise you, or rather that it recognised you, but was careful not to express any surprise. You cannot seriously believe that it is harbouring a grudge against you, or even that it is thinking of something else. It is simply that, like a cow, like a stone or water, it doesn't have anything in particular to say to you. It is looking at you out of courtesy, because you are looking at it.

You pull up the corners of your eyes, to make yourself look Chinese, you try pulling a few faces, eyes bulging: the one-eyed man with the twisted mouth, the monkey with the tongue pushing out the upper or the lower lip, cheeks sucked in, cheeks puffed out. But, Chinese or grimacing, the cow in the cracked mirror just lets you get on with it and does not react. Its docility is so blatant that it reassures you at first, before starting to bother you, for, at length, it does indeed become almost embarrassing. You can lower your eyes before a man or before a cat, because men and cats look at you, and their look is a weapon (and a benevolent look is perhaps the most dangerous of weapons, for it can succeed in disarming you where hatred would fail), but nothing is more discourteous than to lower your eyes before a tree, or before a cow, or before your reflection in the mirror.

Long ago, in New York, a few hundred yards from the groynes where the last Atlantic breakers wash ashore, a man let himself die. He was a penpusher with a law firm. Hidden behind a screen, he remained seated at his desk and never moved. He fed himself on ginger biscuits. He stared out of the window at a wall of blackened brick, which he could almost reach out and touch. It was useless to ask him to do anything, to check a text or go to the post office. Neither threats nor entreaties had any effect on him. Eventually he became almost blind. They had to sack him. He set up home on the stairs of the office block. They had him locked away, but he sat down in the prison courtyard and refused to eat.

YOU ARE NOT DEAD and you are no wiser.

You have not exposed your eyes to the sun's burning rays.

The two tenth-rate old actors have not come to fetch you, hugging you so tightly that you formed a unity which would have brought all three of you down together had one of you been knocked out.

The merciful volcanoes have paid you no heed.

What a marvellous invention man is! He can blow on his hands to warm them up, and blow on his soup to cool it down. He can, if he is not too disgusted, take delicately between his thumb and forefinger any butterfly he chooses. He can cultivate plants and extract from them his food, his clothing, a few drugs, and even perfumes to mask his unpleasant smell. He can beat metals and make saucepans out of them (something a monkey could never do).

So many exemplary stories glorify your greatness and your suffering! So many Robinsons, Roquentins, Meursaults, Leverkühns! The exemplary illustrations, the fine images, the lies: it is not true. You have learnt nothing, you could never bear witness. It isn't true, don't believe them, don't believe the martyrs, the heroes, the adventurers!

Only idiots can talk of Man, Beast, Chaos, and keep a straight face. In order to survive, the most ludicrously tiny insect invests as much, if not more energy than that expended by goodness knows which aviator – a victim of the crazy schedules imposed by the Company to which, moreover, he felt proud to belong – in flying over some mountain which was far from being the highest on the planet.

The rat, in his maze, is capable of truly heroic feats: by judiciously connecting the pedals he has to press in order to obtain his food to the keyboard of a piano or the console of an organ, the animal can be persuaded to give a passable rendition of "Jesu Joy of Man's Desiring", and there is no reason to doubt that he takes great pleasure in doing so.

But, poor Daedalus, there never was a maze. You bogus prisoner! your door was open all the time. There was no warder posted outside, no head-warden stationed at the end of the corridor, no Grand Inquisitor waiting at the garden gate.

It means nothing to talk of hitting rock bottom. Or to plumb the depths of despair or of hatred, or of alcoholic decline or of haughty solitude. The all too perfect image of the diver who resurfaces by pushing off vigorously from the sea bed is there to remind you, if you needed reminding, that the man who has fallen is entitled to all the honours: God's mercy extends no less to him than to those who have never strayed from His flock. Sinners, like divers, are made to be absolved.

But there was no devious-cruising *Rachel* to rescue you from the miraculously preserved wreckage of the *Pequod*, in order that you, another orphan, might bear witness in your turn.

Your mother has not put your new second-hand clothes in order. You are not going to encounter for the millionth time the reality of experience and to forge in the smithy of your soul the uncreated conscience of your race.

No old father, no old artificer will stand you now and ever in good stead.

You have learnt nothing, except that solitude teaches you nothing, except that indifference teaches you nothing: it was a lure, it was a mesmerising illusion which concealed a pitfall. You were alone and that is all there is to it and you wanted to protect yourself; you wanted to burn the bridges between you and the world once and for all. But you are such a neglible speck, and the world is such a big word: all you ever did was to drift around a city, to walk a few kilometres past façades, shopfronts, parks and embankments.

Indifference is futile. It really does not matter whether you wish or you do not wish. You can play pinball or not play pinball, someone, in any case, will come along and slip a twenty centime coin into the slot. You can believe, if you want, that by eating the same meal every day you are making a decisive gesture. But your refusal is futile. Your neutrality is meaningless. Your inertia is just as vain as your anger.

You fondly believe that you are just passing by, indifferent, that you are walking down the avenues, drifting through the city, dogging the footsteps of the crowd, penetrating the play of shadows and cracks.

But nothing has happened: no miracle, no explosion.

With each passing day your patience has worn thinner, the hypocrisy of your pitiful efforts has been laid bare. Time would have had to stand still, but no-one has the strength to fight against time. You may have cheated, snitching a few crumbs, a few seconds: but the bells of Saint-Roch, the changing traffic lights at the intersection between Rue des Pyramides and Rue Saint-Honoré, the predictable drip from the tap on the landing, never ceased to signal the hours, the minutes, the days and the seasons. You may have pretended to forget time, you may have spent nights walking and days sleeping. But you couldn't ever quite get away with it.

For a long time you constructed sanctuaries, and destroyed them: order or inaction, drifting or sleep, the night patrols, the neutral moments, the flight of shadows and light. Perhaps for a long time yet you could continue to lie to yourself, deadening your senses, sinking deeper and deeper into the mire. But the game is over, the great orgy, the spurious exaltation of a life in limbo. The world has not stirred and you have not changed. Indifference has not made you any different.

You are not dead. You have not gone mad.

Disasters do not exist, they are elsewhere. The tiniest catastrophe might have been enough to save you: then you would have lost everything, you would have had something to defend, words of justification to find, words to soften the hearts of your judges. But you are not ill. Your days are not numbered, neither are your nights for that matter. Your eyes can see, your hand does not shake, your pulse is regular, your heart beats. If you were ugly your ugliness might perhaps be fascinating, but you are not even ugly, neither are you a hunchback, a stammerer, an amputee, a legless cripple, you don't even limp.

There is no curse hanging over you. You may be a monster, but not a monster of the lower world. You do not need to writhe in agony, cry out in pain. There is no tribulation in store for you, no rock of Sisyphus, no-one is going to offer you a chalice only to snatch it from your lips at the last moment, there is no crow with sinister designs on your eyeballs, no vulture has been assigned the indigestible chore of tucking into your liver morning, noon, and night. You do not have to grovel before your judges, begging for mercy, imploring their pity. No-one is condemning you, and you have committed no offence. No-one looks at you and then averts their gaze in horror.

Time, which sees to everything, has provided the solution, despite yourself.

Time, that knows the answer, has continued to flow.

It is on a day like this one, a little later, a little earlier, that everything starts again, that everything starts, that everything continues.

Stop talking like a man in a dream.

Look! Look at them. Posted like silent sentinels by the river, along the embankments, all over the rain-washed pavements of Place Clichy, stand thousands upon thousands of mortal men fixed in ocean reveries, waiting for the sea-spray, for the breaking waves, for the raucous cries of the sea-birds.

No, you are not the nameless master of the world, the one on whom history had lost its hold, the one who no longer felt the rain falling, who did not see the approach of night. You are no longer the inaccessible, the limpid, the transparent one. You are afraid, you are waiting. You are waiting, on Place Clichy, for the rain to stop falling.

www.vintage-classics.info